"This is not precisely the meeting I had hoped for."

Guardian angel Major Cuthbert Dunstan Lacy perched on the back of Jamie's carriage.

"Be thankful there was a meeting at all," Eleazar replied wearily. "I had the devil's own time getting him back to England. I thought we'd lose the lovely widow then, but she inveigled James into escorting her to London."

"Ah, but she looks like an angel, and he is, after all, only a man. Still, I think the infatuation has run its course. Did you not notice he was most uncomfortable presenting her to Serena? The problem is, he feels responsible for the lady now, and she, I fear, will play on that."

"Try to encourage Serena," Eleazar said softly. "She must not lose faith in James. I will do what I can, but do not expect miracles."

Cuthbert watched Serena bravely saying goodbye to James as though her heart were not breaking. Of what use was Heaven if it couldn't produce a miracle or two when needed?

Regency England: 1811-1820

*"It was the best of times,
it was the worst of times...."*

As George III languished in madness, the pampered and profligate Prince of Wales led the land in revelry and the elegant Beau Brummel set the style. Across the Channel, Napoleon continued to plot against the English until his final exile to St. Helena. Across the Atlantic, America renewed hostilities with an old adversary, declaring war on Britain in 1812. At home, Society glittered, love matches abounded and poets such as Lord Byron flourished. It was a time of heroes and villains, a time of unrelenting charm and gaiety, when entire fortunes were won or lost on a turn of the dice and reputation was all. A dazzling period that left its mark on two continents and whose very name became a byword for elegance and romance.

Books by Jeanne Carmichael

HARLEQUIN REGENCY ROMANCE

56—A TOUCH OF BLACKMAIL
67—QUEST FOR VENGEANCE
75—A MOMENT OF MADNESS
90—MADCAP JOHNNY

A MATCH MADE IN HEAVEN

Jeanne Carmichael

Harlequin Books

TORONTO • NEW YORK • LONDON
AMSTERDAM • PARIS • SYDNEY • HAMBURG
STOCKHOLM • ATHENS • TOKYO • MILAN
MADRID • WARSAW • BUDAPEST • AUCKLAND

For my beloved cousin Gayle, in memory of
little Miss Loni,
and for my dearest friend, Angie,
in memory of Jerry.
May they soar on the wings of angels.

Published June 1993

ISBN 0-373-31199-0

A MATCH MADE IN HEAVEN

PROLOGUE

"YOU ARE her guardian angel," Eleazar said, sitting easily astride a long beam that ran the length of the high ceiling in the Trevelyan drawing-room, and looking down at the cozy group below.

His companion, not yet accustomed to his spiritual body, clutched the side of the beam as though his life depended upon it. He disliked high places intensely, and abhorred eavesdropping. Indeed, almost everything about his present position disturbed him.

Retired Major Cuthbert Dunstan Lacy was not the sort of man to question orders, and he knew he was in a precarious situation at best. Under ordinary circumstances he might have kept his mouth buttoned, but the sheer lunacy of his assignment, and the growing notion that someone had blundered badly, prompted him to speak.

"I very much fear there has been some mistake," he murmured quietly to his companion. "I know absolutely nothing about babes and even less about females. Why in Heaven's name would they place her in my charge?"

Eleazar, with the knowledge of the ages shining in his clear blue eyes, permitted himself the smallest of smiles. "You may be very sure Heaven knows what it is about."

"Yes, of course," Cuthbert agreed hastily. "I did not mean to imply otherwise. I suppose I should have expected something of this nature—being on probationary status, I mean.''

"I assure you that has nothing to do with your assignment. Those who are in charge of such matters have chosen carefully, and no doubt have reasons far beyond your comprehension for their choice. You may think you are unqualified, but Heaven, in its infinite wisdom, has decreed that you are the ideal angel to have charge of her. For better or worse.''

"I fear it will be for the worse," Cuthbert said with a sigh.

"Well, only time will tell, but if it is any comfort, Heaven's record is rather good. I can only recall one or two mistakes in the last hundred years or so. That fellow they assigned to little Marie Antoinette—poor bit of planning, that. I suspect someone mishandled the incident, but there is nothing in your Serena's chart like that. Some problems, of course, but if you do your job properly, she will live most happily.''

Cuthbert blocked an uncharitable thought from his mind. He had seen for himself his own ledger sheets and been appalled at how nearly balanced the pages were. It was incredible how thorough a record was kept. One more unkind thought, word, or deed and he would never have entered Heaven's gates—even as a probationer.

He glanced down at the intimate group near the fireplace. His charge, an infant girl, lay in her swaddling clothes for all to admire.

"Cheer up, Cuthbert. She's a lovely little thing.''

"It's only that I had hoped for some young man bound for the military," he explained. "Then I might have been of some help.''

"If it is a battle you are seeking, you need not look far," Eleazar answered softly, pointing to Lady Lynton. "She will do everything in her power to block us."

"What? I thought you said Serena was born to love her son—that the charts showed these two were destined for each other."

"So they are," Eleazar agreed calmly, his attention on six-year-old James, who was his own special charge. The lad stood near the cradle, gazing in awe at the baby. "If the pair of them make the right choices, they will have nothing to worry about. Our job is to see that they do. We must always urge them in the correct direction."

"But they cannot see us, and there is little we can do—"

"Nonsense! Have you forgotten your training so soon? I admit we are constrained by certain limitations, but there is still much we are capable of achieving. From this day forward, your charge will hear and recognize your voice. She may refer to it as her 'conscience,' a favourite ploy of mortals, or perhaps as her better self, but she will definitely hear you."

"So they said," Cuthbert replied morosely, peering down at the babe now letting forth a lusty cry. "But they also told us our charges may choose to ignore us completely."

"True, and I confess I am always amazed at the idiocy of...well, let us not speak of that. Just remember that in certain situations, particularly if your Serena is in peril, you have the discretion of using an irresistible impulse to direct her actions. Of course, that is not to be abused and must only be employed in rare instances, but you are familiar with the rules by now, I assume?"

Cuthbert nodded and recited, " 'The ultimate choice must be theirs. We are only here to guide and protect them.' I know the rules, but I don't see the point of it all."

"The point is that Heaven must be earned, Cuthbert, and it is earned through the acts, choices, and decisions one makes while on Earth."

The major gestured to the group below. "Then why not just let them go their way and allow the chips to fall where they may?"

"Cuthbert, Cuthbert, have you learned nothing? Leave these mortals to their own devices and Heaven would be empty. There is evil lurking in the world—evil with most persuasive powers to tempt poor souls and keep them from their destined place in Heaven. Even with guardians, many are lost forever. Still, we must do what we can, but it will not be easy, Cuthbert, and we must pray we shall be successful."

"And if not?" the major asked, not certain he really wished to hear the answer.

"Then each of them will live a quite hellish existence—if you will pardon the expression."

CHAPTER ONE

"LOUISA!" Lady Trevelyan cried, crossing the room in rapid strides to embrace her elder sister.

"Marjorie, at long last. Oh, my dear, how splendid this is!" Louisa Poole, the Countess of Marcham, gathered her younger sister in a crushing embrace, tears misting her eyes.

Serena Trevelyan waited by the door, watching the meeting between her mother and her aunt with frank curiosity. She had never met her Aunt Louisa, but decided instantly that the lady bore little resemblance to the she-dragon Papa described. Indeed, her aunt looked markedly like Mama, except perhaps her dark brown hair had more grey in it, and her heart-shaped face a few more wrinkles.

Lady Trevelyan sniffed and drew back, her own eyes suspiciously moist. She motioned to her daughter. "Come here, Serena, and say hello to your Aunt Louisa."

Lady Marcham turned to observe her niece and blinked back a fresh onslaught of tears. "Why, Marjorie, she is the image of you at seventeen!"

"Not quite," her sister said, smiling. "Serena is much more forward than I ever thought of being! I suppose Laurence and I have rather spoiled her."

The sisters shared a commiserating glance. Both had wanted large families and had spent countless hours of their childhood dreaming of the children they would have and selecting their names. But Louisa had never been able to conceive, and Marjorie had produced Serena only after three miscarriages and two barren years when she thought never to have a child at all. It was little wonder she doted on her daughter.

"I am so pleased to meet you, Aunt Louisa," Serena said, standing before her, her large brown eyes studying the older woman with an air of inquisitiveness that had her mother biting her lip.

"Not nearly so pleased as I, I'll wager," Louisa said gently, and took both of Serena's hands in her own. "Pretty as a picture and just like your mama. Lord, how it takes one back. But what am I thinking of to keep you standing here still in your hats? Serena, my dear, Annie is going to be your maid while you are here. She'll show you up to your bedchamber, and after you have put off your things, she will bring you back here for a nice cup of reviving tea." She nodded towards a shy young girl who stood waiting near the door, and then added with concern, "Unless, of course, you would prefer to rest? I know how fatiguing a long drive can be."

"Oh, I am not in the least tired," Serena assured her, and grinned at her newly acquired maid. "Hello, I'm Serena Trevelyan. I have never had my own maid before, so you must tell me how to go on. Have you always lived in London? It seems so huge, but I vow it must be vastly exciting."

Lady Trevelyan listened to her daughter's artless chatter as Serena followed Annie from the room, and wondered again if she'd made a mistake in bringing her to London.

"I see what you mean," Louisa said with a laugh, linking her arm in her sister's and following at a more leisurely pace. "When I recall how scared to death we were at her age—but she is quite refreshing and at least we need not fear she will become tongue-tied if anyone so much as glances in her direction."

"Not Serena. If anything, she is much more apt to blurt out whatever she is thinking and embarrass you terribly. I do not know but that Laurence may have the right of it, and we should have waited another year to bring her out. She is still such an innocent."

"All the more reason to get her properly settled before she fills her head with a lot of foolish notions."

Marjorie prayed Louisa was right, but when her sister had left her in the spacious bedchamber, she was beset by doubts and wished again that Laurence had come to Town with her, or that she had remained safely at home in Malmesbury. If only Serena did not have that ridiculous fixation. Still, she had behaved very well the last year, so perhaps she was at last getting over it, and London was certain to give her thoughts a new direction.

SERENA, FOR HER PART, was delighted with her new surroundings. Just being in London was enough to set her pulse racing with anticipation. She knew, just *knew* with every ounce of her being, that she would see Jamie before much longer. She danced round the room, flitting from the elegant bookcases to the pretty dressing-table to the window overlooking the square, with small cries of delight at each new discovery.

Annie watched her with amusement and the beginnings of a slavish adoration. She had never seen anyone as exquisite as her tiny charge. To her mind, everything about Miss Serena was perfect. She envied the cloud of waist-length dark hair that fell in shining waves, and the large brown eyes that sparkled beneath dark curly lashes whenever the girl smiled—which was most of the time. Well, she'd smile, too, if she had perfect lips like Miss Serena's which opened to reveal a neat line of tiny white teeth instead of her own crooked ones that sometimes ached alarmingly. Without thinking, her tongue sought out the loose tooth that had been troubling her of late and probed against it, causing a wave of pain to shoot through her.

Annie bit her lip and tried not to think about it. She carefully hung up Serena's cloak before helping her out of her travelling dress and into a white muslin gown with delicate yellow checks. Then she deftly laced the bright yellow ribbon that ran beneath the bosom and tied it in a large bow in the back, thinking it a shame the styles had changed and no longer showed off a lady's figure. Miss Serena had such a tiny waist, but it was hidden beneath the long smooth lines of the dress as it fell from the bosom to her ankles. Not that it mattered, she looked a treat, though not very stylish.

Annie studied her, her head tilted to one side. "Should I put your hair up, miss?"

Serena hesitated. She'd never worn her hair up, but she was entitled to, now that she was making her comeout. The idea was intriguing, but she knew it would take Annie some time and she was too impatient to remain in her room a minute longer than was necessary. "Thank you, but not just yet," she said with a sweet smile. "Perhaps before dinner. I am anxious to speak with my aunt. You will not credit it, I am sure, but I have never seen her before today."

"You don't say," Annie murmured, brushing out the curls and liking the feel of the silky waves beneath her hand. She herself had scores of relatives she'd never seen, and had no wish to see, but then she wasn't Quality like her young lady.

"Mama hasn't seen her in twenty years," Serena confided, moving slightly in her chair, for she could never bear to be still for long. "Mama married against her family's wishes, though what Grandfather had against Papa I cannot imagine, for he is truly wonderful and Mama says he *cherishes* her. I should think that is quite a good thing to have in a marriage and much more important than how wealthy a person may be, but Mama says in Grandfather's time a young lady did not disobey her father, no matter how much in love she might be, and he never forgave her. I think if a young lady loves a gentleman very much, she should be allowed to marry him. Do you not agree?"

"Yes, miss," Annie replied dutifully, though she had never given the matter any thought.

"He would not allow Aunt Louisa to see her either, which I think shows a rather spiteful nature, and though Mama says it is wrong to be glad he died last year, I cannot be very sorry. I asked our vicar and he said I must strive to forgive Grandfather and pray for his soul, and I... Annie, whatever is the matter? You looked very queer just then," Serena said, catching sight of her maid's tortured reflection in the looking-glass.

"It's nothing, miss," she replied, biting sharply on her tongue and closing her eyes for a moment until the pain receded.

Serena was up in an instant and put a comforting arm about the taller girl's waist, leading her to the bed and ordering her to sit.

"Oh, I couldn't, miss. Lady Marcham wouldn't like it above half," she murmured, holding her aching jaw in her hand.

"Nonsense," Serena said, practically pushing her onto the bed. "Anyone with a grain of sense can see you've a toothache, and I know there is nothing worse. How long has it been hurting?"

"Nearly a month, but it's real loose and I expect it will be falling out soon," Annie replied, and then, to her embarrassment, felt hot tears welling up in her eyes. She had endured much without a whimper in her short life, but Serena's gentle compassion was her undoing and the sudden tears overflowed.

"Oh, you poor dear," Serena said, proffering her own handkerchief. "We must have that tooth pulled at once. I shall speak to Aunt Louisa about it as soon as I go down."

"No, you mustn't! You'd only get in trouble yourself and Mrs. Moppit would give me a terrible scold for troubling you."

"Who is Mrs. Moppit?"

"She's the housekeeper and a right tartar. She don't hold with housemaids giving themselves airs and stepping above their station. She'd say I've got no business talking to you."

"Well, she sounds a ninnyhammer. Papa says one's servants are one's responsibility and we must have a care for their health. Now, I am sure I can manage to find my way back to the salon, and you must stay here and rest a bit."

Annie stared up at the tiny lass before her. Miss Serena might look like a fragile flower, but there was no mistaking the look of determination in her eyes. Annie knew there was no point in arguing with her. "Yes, miss," she murmured docilely while planning to resume her duties as soon as the young girl left the room.

"Good, that is settled, then," Serena said, and smiled encouragingly at her maid. "I shall be back as soon as I can." She stepped out of the room, softly shutting the door, and paused for a moment, standing as still as possible and tightly closing her eyes.

The voice came, soft and persuasive, welling up from somewhere deep inside her. *"Well done, Serena."*

She opened her eyes and smiled. The voice was always pleased whenever she did something kind or good and she could usually hear it if she stood quite still and listened for it, but she'd been half-afraid she would not be able to in London—that it might have remained in Malmesbury.

She'd told her mother about the voice once. She was seven at the time, and from her window in the nursery, she'd seen Jamie and two of his friends cutting across Goose Bridge to go fishing. The voice had instructed her to follow him, and Serena had obeyed. She'd fallen into the river that day, but of course Jamie had saved her and she hadn't minded a bit, though Mama had scolded terribly. Serena had tried to explain about the voice then, but Mama hadn't believed her. She'd said it was just her imagination. Serena knew better. It was the voice that had urged her to come to London and told her she would see Jamie soon. Of course, she couldn't tell anyone that, but it was comforting to know it was still with her. With renewed confidence that she was acting for the best, Serena hurried downstairs.

LADY TREVELYAN was down before her daughter and comfortably ensconced in a large armchair drawn near the fire, for though it was April, there was still a chill in the air. A lavish tea tray had been brought in and there was nothing more at the moment that she could wish for except for Laurence's presence. She smiled warmly at her sister. "Where is Sylvester? I am anxious to see him again—has he changed greatly? I remember he was such a handsome boy."

"He's no doubt at one of his clubs, but he will join us for dinner and you may judge for yourself. I think he has aged well, but I will warn you that he has added a great deal of weight and his hair has greyed—like my own."

"You still look beautiful to my eyes," Marjorie said, and reached out a hand across the tea service. "It's hard to believe it has been nearly twenty years."

Louisa squeezed her hand lightly and then asked softly, "Was it worth it, my dear? Have you truly been happy?"

Marjorie nodded. "Except for missing you and Mama so dreadfully. When she died, Papa had the solicitor send me a letter and the locket Mama insisted I have. I confess I cried for days because she never saw Serena, and I know she would have loved her dearly. Somehow, I always believed Papa would relent."

"I think, near the end, he wanted to, but by then his pride would not allow it. You remember how stubborn Papa could be," Louisa said with a sigh, and shook her head at the folly of it all before summoning a smile. "But I am glad you have been happy, and Serena is a lovely child. It will be such a delight bringing her out."

"Thank you, my dear, but I must warn you that sometimes Serena can be a trial. Papa may never have acknowledged her, but she inherited his stubbornness. Once she has decided on a course, it is difficult to per-suade her otherwise. That is one of the reasons Laurence allowed me to bring her to Town. Serena has this notion that she is meant to marry our neighbour's son, Lord Lynton, though she has not seen him for years.''

"Viscount Lynton?" Louisa asked, her brows arching in surprise.

"Why, yes. Do you know of him? Our land adjoins Wynyard Park, his estate there, and recently there has been some renovation work done up at the house. The neighbourhood gossips expect him to return home at any time, and Laurence and I thought it might be best to get Serena away.''

"You do not approve of the match, then?"

Marjorie sighed, wondering how best to explain it. "James is an amiable boy, and when his father was alive, he was frequently at our home, but Lady Lynton does not approve of the connection. She is one of those ambitious women, and claims to be descended, on her mother's side, from Henry VIII. You know the sort, Louisa. She still remembers the old scandal, and you may be very sure she would never approve of the daughter of a mere baronet for her son!''

"But if they love each other?"

"Oh, there is nothing like that. 'Tis only a fantasy of Serena's. When they were children, she tagged along after James and rather worshipped him. Unfortunately, his father and Laurence both encouraged her and there was some talk about a match between them. All nonsense, of course. Even then Henrietta disliked the notion, and when George died, she closed up the house and took James abroad. Serena has not set eyes on him since she was fifteen.''

Louisa smiled, recalling her own childhood passion for her singing master. It had, fortunately, passed rapidly, and she was certain Serena's would be forgotten with equal speed. "I predict that after a month in Town, she will have met so many handsome gentlemen that she will not have a thought to spare for poor Lynton," she said in an attempt to reassure her sister.

"I pray so," Marjorie said, extending her cup for more tea. "Serena has not mentioned him of late, but that may well be because she knows I disapprove. Knowing how his mother feels, I could never allow her to wed Lord Lynton, even if he should return her regard. I said my marriage was worth it, Louisa, and I truly mean that, but all the same I should not wish Serena to endure the heartbreak I did."

"You would not disown her?" her sister asked, her eyes troubled.

"I could not, but Lady Lynton would never agree to the connection, and to see another family torn apart as ours was would be more than I could bear. No, it is far better that Serena forget James entirely. Nothing good could ever come of the association."

"Well, do not worry your head over it. There are a number of dashing young men about just at present, and we shall see what can be arranged. Leave it to me."

Marjorie smiled at her sister's confidence. She knew Serena was not to be so easily managed, but it was difficult to explain her daughter's tenaciousness to anyone else. She glanced up at the clatter of heels in the hall and saw Serena poke her head in the door.

"There you are!" the girl cried in relief. "I have been looking all over for you. Goodness, what an immense house you have, Aunt Louisa. There must be dozens of rooms on this floor."

"Did you get lost, Serena? It is rather large, though I promise you will quickly learn your way about. But where is Annie? She was supposed to show you the way down.''

"I left her in my room," she said, coming to sit on the footstool by her mother's chair and meeting her aunt's gaze directly. "The poor girl has a dreadful toothache and was utterly afraid to mention it to anyone. Is there a tooth-drawer nearby? I promised her it should be attended to at once."

"My dear Serena, you must allow my housekeeper to see to such matters. I am sure when the girl has her half day, Mrs. Moppit will arrange for her to have the tooth removed."

"Oh, but Aunt Louisa, you have not seen her. Annie is in such pain, and there is nothing quite so horrid as a toothache. I know Papa would say it is my duty to see that she is attended to at once. Surely there is a tooth-drawer close by?"

"Well, I suppose if Mrs. Moppit is agreeable, she could walk down to Bond Street. I know there is an apothecary there who sometimes will extract a tooth. We, of course, use Charles Dumergue, who treats the Prince Regent, but he is vastly expensive." She turned to her sister. "You will hardly credit it, Marjorie, but it is said that last year the Regent paid him one hundred guineas for his services."

"I doubt we could get Mr. Dumergue to come at once," Serena said, blithely disregarding the cost. "But if you will provide me with a carriage and directions, I shall take Annie to this apothecary."

Lady Trevelyan smothered a laugh at her sister's open astonishment, but said nothing. Louisa might as well learn at the outset what she had let herself in for in insisting on sponsoring Serena.

Louisa, to her credit, tried gentle reasoning. "Serena, I could not possibly allow you to wander round Town alone—"

"Not alone, Aunt Louisa, for my maid would be with me, and your coachman as well. I dare say he knows his way about, so you need not fear I should get lost or anything. Oh, please, say yes, Aunt. The girl is in such agony, and I cannot bear to see anyone suffering so dreadfully."

Louisa lifted her hands helplessly and appealed to Marjorie. "I do not know what to say. Do you permit Serena to concern herself so much with the servants? I leave that sort of thing to Mrs. Moppit, in general, but—"

"We have so few servants, you see," Marjorie replied with a smile. "And Laurence has always believed it is our duty to see to their health and well-being. He would approve, though, of course, here the decision must be yours."

"Mrs. Moppit does not believe in coddling the staff, and they have their half days to attend to this sort of problem," Louisa said doubtfully. "Still, I suppose an exception could be made—"

"Oh, thank you! I knew you would understand," Serena cried, jumping up and dropping a light kiss on her aunt's brow. "I shall just run up and tell Annie to get ready, and if you will have the carriage brought round, I am sure we shall be back before you have even had time to miss us."

Louisa stared as her niece vanished through the door, a slightly dazed look in her eyes. "I fear I am beginning to see what you meant about Serena's will," she murmured with a sigh. "Oh, dear, I suppose I had best tell Mrs. Moppit."

"Louisa, you are not *afraid* of your housekeeper, are you?"

"No... not really. It is only that she has everything perfectly organized and quite dislikes to have her arrangements overset. Sylvester says the house has never been so well-ordered," she explained, crossing to the bell rope and pulling it to summon a footman.

She had a message conveyed to the mews to have the carriage brought to the door and desired Mrs. Moppit to be informed that Annie had been granted permission to visit the apothecary to have a tooth extracted. She had considered, briefly, allowing the housekeeper to believe the maid had merely accompanied Serena on an excursion, but she could not bring herself to behave in quite so cowardly a fashion with Marjorie's eyes upon her.

As she half expected, the housekeeper tapped on the door of the salon a few moments later. "Might I have a word with you, Lady Marcham?"

Mrs. Moppit was a large woman, nearly mannish in appearance for all she was neatly clad in a black bombazine house dress and white mob-cap. She crossed the room with large strides and stood before her mistress, a frown etched on her wide brow. "Burridge tells me you've given Annie the afternoon off. I really must protest, Lady Marcham."

"The poor child has a toothache, Mrs. Moppit."

"So I understand, but that is just the sort of excuse these lazy girls will use to avoid work. If I may say so, you should have allowed me to handle this, my lady, and you may be certain I will have a few words with Annie Phelps when she returns. The idea of her bothering you with such a matter!"

"It was not Annie, but my daughter," Marjorie said quietly, coming to stand beside her sister. "And judging from Serena's description, the girl was in a great deal of pain."

"I see," Mrs. Moppit said through tightly clenched lips. "You have a very kind daughter, Lady Trevelyan, but I hope in the future she will refer such matters to me. It is most important that order and discipline be maintained if the house is to run just as Lord Marcham wishes." She paused, glancing slyly at Louisa. "I could not work in a house where I did not have full control over the staff. Now, if I may be excused, my lady? This has completely upset my schedule."

Louisa nodded, avoiding the woman's eyes, and waited until the door was safely shut before speaking. "There, you see. I knew she would be dreadfully overset."

"She is perfectly horrid, Louisa! How ever did you come to allow her to tyrannize over you? If I were you, I would discharge her at once."

"Oh, my dear, I could not. You have absolutely no idea of the difficulty of finding domestics in London. Why, I doubt I could find a suitable replacement with the Season just beginning—and Mrs. Moppit came highly recommended."

"By whom? The gaoler at Newgate?"

Louisa smiled at that. "Very nearly—Sylvester's mother."

Their eyes met and the sisters giggled, much as they had done as girls. They were still laughing when Lord Marcham strolled in a few moments later. He greeted his sister-in-law warmly, kissing her on both cheeks, and then took the chair next to his wife.

"How pleasant it is to come home and hear laughter in the house again. I can see this visit is going to agree with Louisa."

"Thank you, Sylvester," Marjorie said, hiding her astonishment at his girth. Louisa had not exaggerated when she said he'd put on weight, and it all seemed to have gone to his middle. But he had the look of a contented man, and the blue eyes she remembered still held the same humorous glint. "It is most kind of you to have Serena and me to stay," she added.

"It is our pleasure, but where is the child? I am anxious to make her acquaintance. If she is anything like the pair of you when you were girls, launching her will be the easiest thing in the world."

"She should be back in a few moments," Louisa said before Marjorie could explain Serena's absence. "Tell us, dear, what is the latest news at the clubs?"

"Jackson won the boxing exhibition, exactly as I predicted—"

"Sylvester!" Louisa scolded. "You know that is not the sort of news we wish to hear."

He grinned, hugely enjoying his little joke. "No, my dear? Well, let's see, then. I ran into old Chelmford at White's, and word is Lewes and Margate are both in Town and Freddie is opening up Palmer House. Got two or three girls to get off this year. You might call on Lady Palmerston, Louisa. Her youngest girl should be about the same age as Serena." He paused, drawing out his pipe, and smiled at his sister-in-law. "Do you recall Lady Palmerston, Marjorie? I believe you are of an age."

"Heavens, it has been so long since I have been in Town, I doubt I shall know anyone."

Sylvester laughed and patted her hand kindly. "Don't concern yourself, my dear. Louisa knows everyone worth knowing, and if it's any comfort, there will be one familiar face in the crowd. I heard a neighbour of yours is in Town—Lord Lynton."

Marjorie visibly paled. "James is here? I thought he was returning to Wynyard Park."

Sylvester, intent on filling his pipe, didn't notice her pallor. "Ha! The lad sent his mama home to oversee renovations there while he kicks up a bit of a lark here. Managing female, his mama. I thought it wouldn't be long before he escaped her clutches. Kept him on too tight a rein, if you was to ask me. Now he's tangled up with some widow lady he met in Paris. Escorted her back to Town, and the gossip-mongers are frothing at the mouth."

CHAPTER TWO

"I BELIEVE IT IS TIME we called on Lady Fitzhugh," Louisa announced several days later, just as they were leaving the elegant home of Mrs. Lowensen.

Lady Trevelyan nearly stumbled on the step of the carriage, and it was only the quick action of the footman, who reached out a steadying hand, that saved her. She thanked him instinctively, but her poise was badly shaken and it was several moments before she could trust her voice sufficiently to question her sister.

"Lady Fitzhugh? I have not thought of her in years and would certainly enjoy seeing her again, but have you forgotten that Serena has another fitting this afternoon?"

"We have time," Louisa assured her, and waited to see if Marjorie would invent yet another reason for delaying the visit. Her sister merely nodded agreeably and glanced out the carriage window as though the matter was of little concern, but Louisa was not deceived.

She knew Marjorie feared seeing Lady Fitzhugh again—and why. Of all the people in Town, Maria was the one most certain to recollect the old scandal. Louisa had told her sister Lady Fitzhugh would never hold it against her, or indeed, even mention the incident. But Marjorie had not been reassured. Louisa had anticipated an argument today, and been ready to counter it, because Lady Fitzhugh was the one person likely to have the information they needed, and something must be done to help Marjorie.

She had seen the anxious way her sister scanned every drawing-room they entered, and her relief at ascertaining Lord Lynton's absence was apparent in the easing of the taut lines about her sister's mouth. Louisa had tried to make Marjorie see that the viscount's appearance in London was not the disaster she imagined, but her sister remained unconvinced. She was certain Serena's Season would be ruined and the girl would not so much as look at another gentleman did she but know Lynton was in Town.

If this continued, Marjorie would not enjoy her visit at all, and Louisa so wanted her to have a splendid time. It was the only way she knew to atone for her silence all these years. A stronger person might have defied Papa and written to a much-loved younger sister, but Louisa had not dared. She bitterly regretted her cowardice now and was quite determined to make amends by bringing Serena out and seeing to it that Marjorie enjoyed all the delights London had to offer. Only this business with the viscount would spoil everything. Well, if anyone knew what Lynton was about, it would be Lady Fitzhugh.

"I dare say she has changed a great deal," Marjorie said at last, unconsciously twisting the strings of her reticule.

"An understatement, darling—only wait till you see her," Louisa said with a laugh. "Why, she has become almost an institution in London, and there is nothing occurring among the ton that escapes her notice." She reached a comforting hand across to her sister. "Marjorie, my dear, I cannot bear to see you so worried.

Maria would be the last person in the world to think ill of you."

Marjorie had no opportunity to answer, as the carriage came to a halt, but she gave Louisa a tentative smile as they stepped out. "I am not so conceited as to believe everyone would still recall my one small rebellion. I should not be surprised if I were forgotten within a fortnight."

"Three days, my dear," Louisa said, leading the way. "A three-day wonder it was."

"That puts me properly in my place," Marjorie murmured as the door opened.

Lady Marcham, a frequent caller in King Charles Street, was recognized instantly by the portly butler. She and her sister were shown to a sitting-room and begged to wait while he informed Lady Fitzhugh of their arrival. Louisa agreed politely, but Marjorie was too enthralled by the room to even notice the butler's departure.

Louisa, too long accustomed to the salon to be dazzled, watched her sister's reaction with amusement. Done in every shade of purple and trimmed with brilliant slashes of scarlet, the room resembled something out of a dream. Or a nightmare, Lord Marcham had been heard to remark. The crowning *pièce de résistance* was an enormous wallpaper panel of fire-breathing dragons that decorated one entire wall.

Marjorie stared at it until recalled to her surroundings by a deep, throaty voice.

"My dear, what an unexpected pleasure this is," Lady Fitzhugh said, sailing majestically across the room with outstretched hands to greet Louisa.

Lady Marcham smiled, returned an airy kiss, and gestured towards Marjorie. "I have brought you a surprise, Maria. You do remember my little sister?"

"Good heavens—is it really you? But of course I should have recognized the name at once. Sir Laurence Trevelyan was the gentleman for whom you threw away a dukedom. Oh, my dear, I fear his grace has never forgiven you. Such a blow to his consequence, you know."

There was little point in taking offence with Lady Fitzhugh and, in truth, Marjorie was too stunned by the lady's appearance to do ought but smile confusedly, for Maria was nearly as wide as she was tall. Marjorie hid her astonishment behind polite inanities and vowed to take her sister to task for not giving her some warning of what she might expect.

Lady Fitzhugh was amused. "Changed a bit, haven't I? No, don't hide your teeth, my dear. I assure you I know well enough what I look like. Come and be seated beside me and Gibbons will arrange for some refreshments while we have a pleasant cose. Gracious, you have barely changed at all. However did you manage to keep your figure?"

While the sisters settled themselves comfortably among the deep cushions, Lady Fitzhugh arranged for tea to be served and Marjorie had ample time to observe her. Maria Anne Delacourt had been a stunning widow the year of Marjorie's first London Season. A slender brunette with nothing much to recommend her save a pair of bewitching eyes and a seductive smile, she'd set the ton on its ear when she had brought the vastly wealthy Lord Fitzhugh up to the mark. But the once sylphlike figure had now disappeared beneath enormous rolls of fat; her smile, no longer holding the lure of Circe, was one of tolerant amusement; her dark eyes seemed lost in the pudgy face and held only a glimmer of the liveliness that had once enchanted dozens of young gentlemen.

"Well?" she demanded abruptly.

"I beg your pardon, Lady Fitzhugh," Marjorie stammered, somewhat flustered at being caught staring.

"Don't colour up, my dear. There'd be no point in wearing these outlandish fashions if they didn't make people stop and give me a second look. I like a bit of attention, you know," she said, and chuckled deeply, the folds of her skin shaking beneath the double chins and the ostrich plumes adorning her scarlet turban bobbing alarmingly.

Marjorie smiled. Impossible not to, for it was a bit like seeing a mountain move, and she dared not meet Louisa's eyes for fear she'd burst into a fit of giggles. She was saved by the entrance of a pair of pretty housemaids bearing a laden tea tray and numerous dishes of tarts, pastries and candies. Her attention was caught. The golden-haired girls appeared nearly identical, and their dark dresses and white caps provided a startling contrast to the flamboyant viscountess.

Maria was watching her. "Have to give the gentlemen something pleasant to look at," she said. "Tea? Or will you join me in a glass of champagne?"

"Tea, please," Marjorie managed to utter, once again disconcerted by Lady Fitzhugh's ability to read her mind.

"I have come to terms with my life, my dear. I hope you have—no sense in repining for what is lost. I have been telling your sister that for years."

It was Louisa's turn to be flustered, and her delicate fingers trembled against the fine china cup. "It is not as easy for some of us, Maria, but you will own I have made a start in persuading Marjorie to visit."

"There, pet, I never meant to distress you," Maria said, her voice unexpectedly soft. She glanced at Marjorie, adding, "Louisa and I share a bond. Barren, the pair of us." She shrugged her massive shoulders. "I accepted long ago that it simply was not meant to be, but Louisa somehow blames herself and tries endlessly to make it up to Marcham for not providing him an heir. Not that he cares a rap, one way or the other, though you will never convince her of that!"

"Please, Maria," Louisa interrupted. "We did not come to discuss my troubles."

"Oh, very well," she replied, sipping her champagne and watching her friend from over the rim of the glass. There were few people in London she truly cared deeply for, but Louisa Poole was one of them, and she would willingly do what she could to help the lady. "I suppose it is that pretty niece of yours you wish to discuss. I am told she is a beauty. What is she called? Serena, is it?"

Louisa nodded, but Marjorie stared in astonishment. Serena had been kept close to the house, save for her fittings. Louisa did not want her seen until she was properly clothed, but Lady Fitzhugh had apparently already heard reports of the child.

"The truth is, Maria, we are a little worried. Marjorie believes Serena to be infatuated with a young gentleman and had hoped a Season in London would help her to forget him. Unfortunately, we have heard the gentleman—Lord Lynton—is recently arrived in Town."

"Ah, now this is interesting. I had thought it was something simple you wanted, like vouchers."

"That, too," Louisa said with a smile. "If you will use your influence with the patronesses, I shall be indebted to you. However, that can wait till after her court presentation. I have told Marjorie if anyone in Town knows the latest gossip, it is you."

"To be sure, my dear. So she is enamoured of Lynton, is she? Well, the child has excellent taste and it would not be a misalliance. What is the problem?"

Marjorie blushed at such plain speaking, and Louisa answered for her. "Lady Lynton does not approve the connection. My sister fears that even if the gentleman were to return Serena's regard, which is not at all certain, his mother would not countenance the match and it would create a rift in the family."

"I see," Maria said slowly, her pudgy, bejewelled hand tapping idly against the table. "Well, my advice would be to consign Lady Lynton to the devil—I never liked the woman above half—but I suspect that will not appeal to you."

She leaned back against the cushions of her chair. "Lynton. Let me see. Devilishly handsome gentleman…there was something I heard recently. Oh, yes— he's taken up with a widow he met in Paris, and a pretty piece of work she is! She is English by birth, so I understand, but has a French air about her, and a marked disrespect for our customs. I heard Lynton escorted her to Town and is living in her pocket, much to his mama's consternation. He sent *her* home, so the widow's hold over him must be fairly strong. I shouldn't worry about your Serena running into him. Mrs. Tallant will not be received save on the fringes of the ton."

"Well, that is a relief. Marjorie was half-afraid to al-low Serena out of the house for fear she would meet him."

"Not anywhere your daughter is likely to go, Lady Trevelyan," Maria said with another of her deep-throated chuckles. "But I will promise you this. By the time the Widow Tallant is finished with young Lynton, his mama will be wishing she'd had the good sense to throw him at Serena."

WHILE HER MOTHER was discussing the possibility of her encountering Lord Lynton, Serena was chafing at the restraints placed up on her. She was not allowed outside the house except for a series of what seemed like endless fittings or a brief stroll round the square with Annie in attendance. It was poor exercise for a young lady accustomed to long, rambling walks in the coun-try or bruising rides over the fields of Malmesbury. Serena longed for her horse, especially on so pretty an April morning.

She was sitting in the breakfast parlour, still looking wistfully out the window and feeling unaccountably melancholy, when her uncle joined her.

"Good morning, Serena. Lovely day, what?" he asked, taking his seat at the table and unfolding his copy of the *Morning Chronicle*.

"Yes, Uncle," she replied quietly, for she had al-ready learned he liked to read his paper in peace and did not enjoy conversation until he had quite finished his breakfast.

Something in her voice, however, gave him pause, and he lowered his paper to glance across the table at her. "You sound a trifle downcast, Serena. Are you missing your home a bit? I dare say London must seem rather daunting at first, but you'll soon grow accustomed."

Serena smiled. "I fear I have not seen enough of London to be daunted as yet! But I do not mean to complain and Aunt Louisa has perfectly explained why I must not yet be seen abroad . . . only it is such a beautiful morning. It seems a dreadful waste to spend it indoors."

"And what would you be doing on such a day in Malmesbury?"

"Riding, I expect," she said, her eyes brightening at the thought. "Papa bought me the most splendid bay and she is just now learning to properly take a jump. I call her Buttercup and she is the dearest, cleverest horse in the world."

Sylvester watched her indulgently, deciding his niece was a taking little thing. There was an animation about the child quite lacking in most of the young ladies of his acquaintance. He put a question to her about her horse solely for the pleasure of seeing her eyes light up as she chattered. Serena answered him sensibly, however, and then enquired about the parks in London and whether riding might be permitted. Sylvester laid aside his paper and was explaining the rules of the various parks when an idea suddenly occurred to him.

"I say, Serena, how would you like a tour? A morning drive through the parks?"

"Oh, Uncle Sylvester, could we? I should like it above all things—only Aunt Louisa said I must not be seen just yet."

"And you are not likely to be at this hour, my dear. I see no harm in it. Fetch your hat and coat, then, and as soon as I have finished here we shall be off."

Serena skipped round the table and dropped a grateful kiss on his forehead. "It is indeed kind of you and I shall try not to plague you with questions, which my aunt says you dislike excessively."

"Saucy puss," he murmured as she disappeared, but he was smiling broadly and feeling absurdly pleased with himself for providing the child with a bit of pleasure.

Serena did not keep him waiting long, and he thought her appearance did him credit, though even he knew her dress to be sadly outdated. Its high neck, lacy collar, and long sleeves proclaimed her a provincial, and the bonnet she wore with it was decidedly out of fashion. Still, he thought on the whole his niece looked rather sweet, and he gallantly offered his arm.

He had ordered the curricle brought round, explaining to Serena that she would have a much better view and that it would not be as stuffy as the Town coach. The truth was, the unusually warm and sunny weather had affected him as well, and he was not at all averse to taking his team out. Serena applauded his decision, complimented him on his showy chestnuts, and settled herself on the seat, fully prepared to enjoy herself.

Sylvester nodded to the boy holding his horses and the lad stepped aside smartly. With expert timing, he swung up on the perch behind them as the curricle swept past and grinned at Serena as she twisted her neck round to watch him.

Satisfied the groom was safely aboard, Serena turned to her uncle. "Why ever do Londoners call their groom a tiger?"

"Well, there you have me," he said, looking surprised. "I have never given the matter thought. You may as well ask why the sun is called the sun." He chuckled at his wit before turning his attention to his horses.

Serena, already distracted by some of the fine houses they were passing, longed to ask him dozens of questions. She remembered her promise, however, and sat quietly, giving only an occasional little cry of surprise. She was able to contain her curiosity fairly well—at least until they turned onto Pall Mall. On that vast cobbled street, with its elegant houses, London appeared at its finest.

Sylvester, pleased with her astonishment, slowed the carriage and pointed out the fifteen grand columns that marked the front of Carlton House, where the Prince Regent resided.

"You would blink even harder, my dear, were I to tell you the cost of that edifice. It was rebuilt for Prinny, you know, and no expense spared. The rooms inside are even more magnificent, and decorated in the finest taste. Well, who knows," he said with one of his chuckles, "we may even wangle an invitation for you to attend one of the musicales he gives and you may see the splendour for yourself. A pity you were not here last year when the Regent gave a fête for Wellington. Two thousand guests, my dear. Aye, you may well stare."

It was not, however, the impressive colonnade that had caught Serena's attention, but the three young gentlemen engaged in an animated conversation directly across the street from their carriage. Serena drew in her breath. From the back, one young man, dressed in a tight-fitting blue cutaway coat, reminded her distinctly of Jamie. Then the gentleman turned, and disappointment washed over her. He was a trifle too heavy to be Jamie, his nose too large and his chin too round. She turned back to her uncle with a sigh and agreed with forced enthusiasm to his proposal of driving across Piccadilly and taking a turn about Green Park.

She knew her disappointment was out of reason. She had not really anticipated seeing Jamie this morning. Only the sudden rush of hope, extinguished so rapidly, depressed her spirits.

Her uncle thought her overawed and teased her. "It may seem very grand now, but I will wager a monkey that in less than a month, you will be taking it all for granted and yawning with *ennui* as all the ladies do. It is not considered fashionable to show your amazement, my dear. It will mark you as a green girl just up from the country."

Serena smiled at such nonsense and accepted his hand as he helped her down from the carriage a few moments later. Whatever her disappointment, it would be churlish of her not to show some pleasure when her uncle was at such pains to provide for her enjoyment. She looked about with the air of one willing to be pleased and remarked how very pretty the green looked in the morning sun. "It is aptly named, Uncle."

"Eh? Oh, yes, I suppose so. No flowers in this park, you know. They say it is because the leper women from St. James's Hospital were buried here. No other reason to account for it when they grow in profusion across the way in St. James's Park."

She checked, looking beneath her feet at the smooth green lawn, but Sylvester urged her on.

"I should like you to see the temple, my dear. It was erected during the peace celebrations. Ah, it was something to see. Hundreds of rockets were shot up, Roman candles, Catherine wheels—the most amazing display. And when the smoke had cleared, the temple was revealed. Look there," he said, pointing towards the east.

They had reached the crest of a small hill, and Serena looked in the direction he indicated. Less than a hundred feet away stood a miniature castle, fronted with tall columns, between which hung immense paintings. "Oh, Uncle! It is exquisite!"

"Thought you'd like it," he said, and they strolled a bit closer. "It is called the Temple of Concord. Should you care to stroll round it?"

Serena hesitated. It was truly a work of art and she would have dearly loved to take a closer look, but the small park was beginning to fill with people, and, mindful of her aunt's strictures, she wondered if it would not be wiser to return to the carriage. Her uncle seemed unconcerned, however, and on closer observation it was apparent, even to Serena's untutored eye, that these people were not of the Haut Ton. A few soldiers were present, easily identified by their scarlet coats, but the majority of the persons seemed to be of an unidentifiable class. "Shabby-genteel," Aunt would perhaps say.

They strolled down the hill arm in arm, Sylvester intent on explaining the allegorical pictures and an enthralled Serena observing the passers-by. She inadvertently caught the eye of an obese gentleman, nattily attired in a flamboyant yellow coat that had seen better days and would not quite stretch over his vast stomach. A brilliant green-striped waistcoat was displayed beneath this erstwhile finery, the material worn to a shine and glinting in the morning sun. Serena hastily raised her eyes, only to encounter a knowing wink from the man.

He tipped his hat to her uncle, smiling broadly. "Fine morning for a stroll with your little ladybird, eh, governor?"

The woman with him was nearly as thin as he was stout, and well past her youth. Her hair, a most unnatural shade of red, competed for attention with her heavily rouged cheeks and bright red lips. She essayed a shrill laugh and pulled at his arm. "Come along, Billy boy, do. No need for you to be eyeing another when you've all you can handle right here."

Serena was hard put not to laugh at such an ill-assorted pair, but her uncle was not pleased and abruptly altered their course. "We had best return to the carriage, my dear. I fear Green Park is not what it used to be."

"Oh, Uncle, did you see her hair? Never have I seen such a colour! I vow it was all I could do not to stare. Do you suppose she is an actress?"

"Serena, you will oblige me by putting that—that person out of your mind. She is not at all the sort you should know, and your aunt would have my head on a platter if she knew I had taken you into such ill company."

Serena glanced over her shoulder at the disappearing couple with renewed interest. Could her uncle mean the woman was a . . . bird of paradise? She had never seen such a creature, but Geraldine Richmond had told her of their existence and that gentlemen paid dearly for the pleasure of their company.

"Do not stare, Serena. Such people are beneath your notice," her uncle said, urging her towards the carriage.

Serena studied his profile. She would dearly love to ask him about the woman, but his demeanour was suddenly forbidding and she hastened her steps to match his. They were just nearing the drive where their carriage waited when she saw another lady descending from a barouche, halted directly beside their own. The gentleman assisting her reminded her of Jamie from the back, but she had learned her lesson and knew she must not allow herself to imagine every set of broad shoulders to belong to him. She turned her attention to the lady, watching with interest as she placed a tiny dog on the grass. It was the most absurd thing.

"Look, Uncle Sylvester," she whispered. "Is that not clever? The lady's dog matches her costume."

Sylvester glanced up, relieved at once to see the woman was respectably attired. Indeed, she looked most fetching in a fashionable walking dress. The jacket was maroon, buttoned to the waist, and festooned with gold braid at the shoulders. The skirt was white and fell to a pair of trim ankles, which he glimpsed as she stepped down. The lady's parasol was done in the same shades of maroon and white as her dress, and a delicate white hat was perched on top of her blond head, its ostrich plumes dyed a matching maroon. Very smart.

He glanced then at the dog that had attracted his niece's attention. Ridiculous, he thought, his good opinion of the lady vanishing as he eyed the miniature white hat with tiny maroon feathers tied on the poor animal's head.

The lady, apparently sensing their interest, turned her head and smiled warmly at Sylvester.

He instantly straightened his shoulders, pulled in his girth so far as he was able, and beamed in her direction. Where had this exquisite been keeping herself? Never had he seen such a flawless complexion, or eyes so large and blue. And her mouth—like a rosebud, he thought, and so perfectly formed. It went divinely with the blond curls framing her delicate face.

"Do not be too censorious, sir! I assure you the dog quite enjoys her attire. She is a female, you see," she said with a small laugh, which clearly invited him to share her joke.

At the sound of her voice, the gentleman turned. He was tall and well formed, though perhaps a trifle slender for his height, and moved with a natural grace. Dark golden curls fell across a wide brow above a set of fine deep blue eyes, thickly lashed, and a long, straight nose. His mouth was generous and he had the look of one who smiled easily, though he was just saved from too delicate a face by a strong, square chin.

He nodded courteously to the pair and was about to turn away when Serena suddenly ran the few steps between them.

"Jamie! Oh, Jamie, it is you!" she cried, and hurled herself into his arms.

James Paget Crandall, Viscount Lynton, was knocked back on his heels, though he instinctively clutched at the bundle of femininity in his arms. The small poodle braced its hind legs and yapped furiously, while the young lady with him looked on with tolerant amusement.

"Serena? Is that you? What on earth—here, stop clutching at me and tell me at once what you are doing in London. I thought you still at Malmesbury."

"Oh, Jamie, is it not wonderful?" Serena said, drawing back slightly but not releasing her hold on his arm. "Mama brought me to Town, and I knew I would see you! Oh, it has been such an age and I have missed you so very much."

Sylvester cleared his throat and Serena turned to him at once. "Uncle, this is my dearest friend and I cannot believe our good fortune in meeting him here. But I forget my manners. May I present Ja—I beg your pardon—Lord Lynton? And Jamie, this is my uncle, Lord Marcham. I am staying with him and Lady Marcham.''

James firmly set Serena aside, bowed politely to Lord Marcham, and then drew the other young lady's arm through his own. ''My companion, Mrs. Tallant,'' he said, performing the introduction with a mixture of embarrassment and defiance.

Mrs. Tallant gave her hand to Lord Marcham, smiling at him in such a way as to convey her admiration, and then turned to Serena. ''And your young friend?'' she asked, delicate brows arching and an amused smile playing about her lips.

''May I present Miss Trevelyan?'' he responded, his manner curt. Then, aware of how rude he sounded, he added, ''She is the daughter of our nearest neighbour and I have known her since the cradle, though it has been some years since we last met.''

''Two,'' Serena corrected quietly, stepping away from him. She did not understand his reticence. One might almost believe Jamie was not pleased to see her.

''And no doubt she has been infatuated with you all these years,'' Mrs. Tallant said with her odd little smile. ''What was that you called him, my dear? 'Jamie?' How very sweet.''

Serena smiled dutifully, but her eyes sparkled with anger at the woman's patronizing tone and she had to suppress a very unladylike desire to rearrange Mrs. Tallant's elegant coiffure.

James silently cursed his ill luck at running into Serena here of all places. He had been discreet about appearing in public with the widow. But there was nothing to do but make the best of it. A neatly gloved hand went to his cravat. "Have you been visiting the temple? I promised to show it to Mrs. Tallant and it seems like a fine morning for a drive."

"Indeed, indeed," Sylvester murmured. "Well, we shall not keep you. Pleasure to meet you, Lynton. Your servant, Mrs. Tallant."

"THIS IS NOT precisely the meeting I had hoped for," Cuthbert said from his perch on the back of Sylvester's carriage.

"Be thankful there was a meeting at all," Eleazar replied wearily, climbing up beside him. "I had the devil's own time getting him back to England. I thought we'd lose the lovely widow then, but as soon as she learned his plans, she changed her own and inveigled our James into escorting her to London."

"What's become of Lady Lynton? One would have thought she could be trusted to keep him away from the likes of the widow," Cuthbert asked a bit furiously, for he could not bear to see Serena hurt.

"She tried—oh, indeed she did! Which is why young James sent her home to Wynyard. He does much for his mother, but he won't be managed."

"Oh no? That woman seems to be doing a fair job of it, though I cannot believe he would lose his head over her. Why, anyone with half an eye can see what she is!"

"Ah, but she looks like an angel, and he is, after all, only a man. Still, I think the infatuation has nearly run its course. Did you not notice he was most uncomfortable presenting her to Serena? The problem is, he feels responsible for the lady now, and she, I fear, will play on that."

Sylvester's tiger climbed on the back of the curricle and Eleazar stepped through him, floating just above the carriage. The short groom felt a strange sort of draught and looked round in a confused manner.

Cuthbert, ignoring the tiger, glared up at Eleazar and demanded, "What are we to do, then?"

"Nothing," Eleazar said, and there was note of warning in his voice. "You know the rules, Major! No interference. You have already been warned twice. They must work this out for themselves." There was no reply, and after a moment he added in a softened tone, "Try to encourage Serena. She must not lose faith in James. I will do what I can with him—but do not expect miracles. These things take time."

Cuthbert didn't reply. He watched Serena bravely holding her head up and smiling goodbye at James just as though her heart were not breaking. Of what use was Heaven if it couldn't produce a miracle or two when needed?

CHAPTER THREE

SERENA, initially disappointed by Lord Lynton's luke-warm greeting, soon allowed her inner voice to convince her that Jamie would call on Lady Marcham at the first opportunity. As a consequence, she spent several wretched afternoons waiting for him, and three very long, sleepless nights troubled over his seeming defection. Her faith in Jamie nearly faltered, and not even the delivery of her new gowns and dresses had the power to lift her from her low spirits. Nor had the weather helped; it had rained steadily for two solid days. On Thursday, however, she awoke to find the sun shining brightly, and her naturally optimistic nature returned.

With an inner conviction of Jamie's devotion that defied logic, but which owed much to Cuthbert's persuasive powers, she managed to find several excuses for his strange behaviour and confided them to Annie. "It must be thought quite natural for him to be a trifle reserved. After all, it has been two years since we last met and I dare say I have changed a great deal," she said, studying her face in the looking-glass while Annie brushed her hair.

"Yes, miss."

"And Mrs. Tallant was with him," she continued. "I thought her a bit older than Jamie, so perhaps she is a

friend of Lady Lynton's and he was merely being polite, showing her the temple and all."

"Do you think so, miss?" Annie asked with a trace
of surprise, for she had heard Serena sobbing into her
pillow the night before.

"Oh, I am certain of it and cannot think how I came
to be so silly as to believe otherwise! She is not at all the
sort of lady Jamie would choose as a friend. And now
that I come to consider it, I believe Uncle's presence
most likely made Jamie ill at ease. Do you not think it
likely?"

"Yes indeed, miss."

"It is most odd, Annie, but I do believe Uncle found
Mrs. Tallant attractive...he smiled at her in the
strangest way."

"Gentlemen do behave oddly sometimes, miss,"
Annie said, keeping her opinions to herself. She had
heard the entire tale of the encounter with Lord Lynton from Serena and had no high opinion of Mrs. Tallant, but there was no sense in worrying the young lady.

"There, miss," she said, stepping back after twisting a green ribbon through Serena's curls. "If your
young man was to see you now, he'd soon be forgetting
Mrs. Tallant."

"Oh, thank you, Annie," she said, turning to gaze in
the looking-glass. She thought her coiffure, with its
abundance of curls, childish compared to the smooth
elegance of the widow. But Annie had worked tire-
lessly on it and she smiled at the girl. "My hair has
never looked so pretty before. You do it wondrously
well. Now, where did I put my new reticule?"

"Here it is," Annie said, handing her the tiny green
satin bag that perfectly matched the stripe of her dress.
"Will you be long, miss?"

"I expect so," Serena said. "Aunt Louisa wishes to introduce me to several of her friends. It is very kind of her," she added, but there was little enthusiasm in her voice.

"You go along and enjoy yourself, miss, and if anyone should call, well, no doubt it will do him good to find you not sitting here waiting on his pleasure!"

"Oh, Annie! Jamie is not like that."

"That's as may be, miss, but if you was to ask me, it don't pay to let a gentleman know you are overly fond of him."

"Maybe most gentlemen, but Jamie is different," Serena assured her, readily forgetting the long hours she had waited for him to appear. She had been so certain he would call and so vastly disappointed when he had not. But of course he must have had prior engagements.

She glanced again out the window. The square was still empty and her mama and aunt were waiting belowstairs. "I must go, Annie. Do try to rest a bit while I am gone. You look dreadfully tired today. Are your teeth paining you again?"

"No, miss," Annie said with a smile that revealed the missing tooth. Its removal had been a blessed relief and almost worth the wrath of Mrs. Moppit. She was still paying toll for that afternoon, but she didn't want her young lady to know the trouble she had caused. Not when she had only meant to be helpful.

Serena hesitated, feeling something was amiss, but her mother tapped on the door and looked in. "Are you ready, darling? The carriage is waiting— Oh, how lovely you look!"

"Thank you, Mama," Serena said, and gathering up her gloves, waved to Annie before following her mother down the stairs.

"Charming, utterly charming," Louisa declared as Serena came down the steps. "I knew that green would become you, my dear, and the ribbon in your hair is the perfect touch. Marjorie, do you recall that pretty hat we saw in Oxford Street—the one with the green feathers? I believe it may just match Serena's dress. Perhaps, if we've time this afternoon, we could take another look at it."

"Louisa, I cannot allow it. You have bought Serena so many dresses and hats already, I fear you will bankrupt poor Sylvester."

"Pooh! He can stand the nonsense, my dear, and you must not begrudge me so small a pleasure."

The sisters argued agreeably during the carriage drive and Serena was left to her own thoughts. She imagined meeting Jamie again, only this time she'd be fashionably clad in one of her new gowns and the centre of an admiring group of gentlemen. She could picture his astonishment, so complete he would utterly ignore his companion, Mrs. Tallant, and beg for the privilege of leading Serena out in the quadrille or minuet....

"Serena," her mother said, interrupting her pleasant reverie by tapping her sharply on the arm. "Your aunt is speaking to you. Have your wits gone begging?"

"Oh, I am sorry."

"Do not apologize to me, child. Your mother was just the same at your age. Always wool-gathering. But I pray you will not indulge in daydreams this afternoon. Lady Colchester is a high stickler and will take offence if you do not pay her every observance."

Serena nodded to show she was listening and vowed to put Jamie from her mind. But she couldn't help thinking it would be beyond wonderful if he should put in an appearance at one of the houses they were to visit. Why, Jamie might very well be at Lady Colchester's, she thought, stepping down eagerly from the carriage.

They were shown into an impressive salon. A huge fireplace dominated one end of the room, and though the day was warm, a blazing fire added its heat. The far side of the room was lined with windows, and three alcoves provided cushioned seats for the guests. Near the door, a group of sofas and chairs was arranged about a tea table. Similar seating was provided at intervals along the wall, and small groups of elegantly clad ladies and gentlemen sat sipping tea or strolling about.

It took only a quick glance about the spacious room to be certain Jamie was not present, and Serena turned her attention to her hostess. Lady Colchester was a tall woman who held herself as proudly as any royal princess. Her black hair was drawn sleekly back into a knot of curls and held in place with a large diamond pin. It was her only adornment and added to her regal air. She looked down her long, straight nose at Serena for a moment before inclining her head slightly, indicating they were to be seated.

Behind her, Lady Marcham breathed a sigh of relief. While Lady Colchester did not wield the power of one of the patronesses of Almack's, or even the wealthy influence of Lady Fitzhugh, she was nevertheless one of the fashionable leaders of the ton. Her good opinion would go far in advancing Serena. Now if only her niece could be trusted to keep to the line and not put forward any of her odd opinions, all would be well.

She had instructed Serena carefully. If she should be asked to sit beside Lady Colchester, it would signify instant approval. She was then to listen politely, compliment her hostess if the opportunity arose, and make no effort to initiate any conversation.

Serena thought it all rather like a game and sat quietly, her back as straight as a board and her feet carefully together. While Lady Colchester conversed with her mama and aunt, she surveyed the room. There were half a dozen young ladies in attendance with their mamas, and several gentlemen. Brothers, perhaps coerced into providing escort, Serena thought. She knew that presently new callers would arrive to take the coveted seats by Lady Colchester and then she would be presented to the others in the room. They would circulate slowly, until reaching the door again, at which point they would take their leave. It was all conducted like a well-ordered play.

Serena amused herself imagining what the other young ladies might be like, and though it appeared she was paying strict heed to Lady Colchester's words, she was soon lost in her own world of dreams. Fortunately, no further comments were addressed to her and she was recalled to her surroundings when Aunt Louisa rose a few moments later. Serena curtsied politely, received another nod of approval and moved off between her mama and aunt.

"That went very well," Louisa murmured as they approached two older ladies and a young girl about Serena's age. "Ah, Lady Yarmouth and Mrs. Appleby. How delightful to see you here. May I present my sister, Lady Trevelyan, and her daughter, Miss Trevelyan?"

The introductions performed, the two young ladies
stepped slightly aside to allow their elders to talk. Miss
Appleby was ill named, Serena thought, for she had
never encountered a young lady of such fragile-looking
appearance. No apples in the cheeks here, but an
astonishingly white complexion, lips with just a tinge of
pink, and light blue eyes. Blond hair, so pale it was
nearly white, hung in a soft cloud, completing the
ethereal look of the girl.

The illusion was shattered when Miss Appleby, an
impish smile on her pretty lips, turned to Serena and
whispered, "What an appalling bore this is!"

"I beg your pardon?" Serena said, thinking she
could not have heard correctly.

Miss Appleby stepped into the window enclosure and
drew Serena along with her. "Never tell me you are actually enjoying all this—it is all such a farce. And the
countess is the worst of the lot. La, did you ever see
anyone so high in the instep? I vow it is quite diverting
when you consider her brother."

"I did not know she had a brother," Serena ventured, uncertain how else to respond.

Miss Appleby stared at her. "You have not heard of
Rotterdam? Have you just arrived in Town? My dear,
the earl is notorious. A *rake* with the worst reputation," she whispered, and added with dreamy eyes, "*He*
is the only reason I allowed Mama to persuade me to
come today."

"Oh," Serena replied, with only a vague notion of
what a rake might be, but she instantly recognized the
adoration in Miss Appleby's eyes, and that feeling she
could easily understand. "Well, I shall hope for your
sake that he makes an appearance. Is your acquaintance with him of long standing?"

Miss Appleby laughed aloud, an amusing ripple of sound in the quiet room that instantly brought a disapproving frown from her mama. She turned slightly away and lowered her voice. "We were introduced last year, but I rather doubt he recollects the incident! Rotterdam, my dear, does not pay court to young ladies in their first Season. But this is my second year, and I have hopes that things will be different," she added, a mischievous light in her eyes. "I was such an innocent last year, but one learns, my dear, one learns. I believe I shall know better how to handle him this time—if only I have the opportunity."

Serena was all admiration. Miss Appleby could not be more than a year or so older than herself, but she had a sophisticated air about her that Serena readily envied. "I am certain you will succeed," she said.

"One can but hope. You are very kind, Miss Trevelyan. Shall we cry friends? I am Cressida, though you may call me Cressy if you like."

"I should be pleased to do so, if you will address me as Serena."

"What a pretty name! Indeed, it suits you, for you are a very pretty girl and I wager you will be an instant success and have all the gentlemen clamouring for your attention. Why, I should not be in the least surprised if you are engaged before the Season is half over. Have you met a gentleman you admire? You must confide in me if we are to be friends."

"There is one, but I did not meet him in London," Serena said with a shy smile. "I have known him since the cradle. When I was twelve, he promised to marry me."

"Good heavens! But are you certain of your feelings, my dear? Why, there can be no excitement, no mystery in adoring a man you have known all your life!''

Serena laughed. "I am not seeking excitement and would be vastly content just to be his wife. He is...well, he is just wonderful.''

"A paragon, I perceive. May I know his name?''

"Lord Lynton. He has been abroad and just returned to London. Are you perhaps acquainted with him?''

A shadow crossed Cressy's eyes and she glanced away, remarking casually, "I do not believe we have been introduced, but I have met so many gentlemen of late, 'tis difficult to keep them straight.''

"Jamie is rather tall and—''

"Oh, my stars. It's him!'' Miss Appleby broke in excitedly. ''Whatever shall I do?''

Serena looked towards the door, as did everyone in the room. There was a moment of silence and then the hum of conversation rapidly resumed as the Earl of Rotterdam glanced sardonically about.

He was tall, taller even than Jamie, but not as handsome, Serena thought loyally. Of course, the earl was a great deal older, but there was a harshness about him that she could not admire. It was not just the way his dark eyes raked the room with contempt or the disdainful smile on his lips. His skin was darkly tan, almost swarthy, and a jagged scar blazed down one cheek, giving him a villainous look that not even his well-cut, fashionable clothes could deny. He belonged on a pirate deck with a sword in his hand and the wind ruffling his hair, she thought, her eyes roving over his figure. She smiled, amused by her fantastical thoughts, and glanced up again to find her scrutiny returned by a pair of green eyes. Cat's eyes.

"Good heavens, he's smiling at me," Miss Appleby murmured. She ventured a small wave of her gloved hand, but the earl had turned away to speak with his sister.

"I gather that gentleman is Lord Rotterdam," Serena said softly.

"Is he not magnificent? Oh, whatever shall I say to him? I vow I am all about in the head when he is in the same room, and I cannot think at all clearly," she said, turning her back on the earl and studying the view from the window in an effort to compose herself.

"Perhaps he will not speak to us," Serena said, making an effort to soothe her new friend.

"Do not say so! I shall die if he does not! To see him again, to speak with him—it is what I have been wishing for. Quickly, tell me, Serena, what is he doing now?"

"He is looking in our direction," she replied, and nearly laughed at her friend's sudden shyness. All traces of the sophisticated young lady had disappeared. "I believe you may get your wish, Cressy. He is crossing towards us."

Ivor Gyfford, the fourth Earl of Rotterdam, nodded coolly to one or two ladies of his acquaintance but did not pause to speak. It was such scorn for the polite tenets of Society that had given him a reputation for surliness. He was accustomed to behaving as he pleased, and at the moment, it pleased him to discover the identity of the impudent young lady with Miss Appleby.

His sister, never tiring of her desire to see him respectably settled, had pointed out Miss Appleby's presence. He had glanced in her direction, intending to do no more than give her a passing nod, when he had encountered the humorous eyes of her companion.

Miss Appleby turned at his approach. A blush lent some colour to her pale cheeks and her eyes sparkled brightly as she extended her hand with what she hoped was a modicum of sophistication. "My Lord Rotterdam. How utterly delightful to see you again."

He bowed over her hand. "Your servant, Miss Appleby. Have you just returned to Town?"

"A week ago, my lord, and I vow I am bored to tears. La, it is all so very fatiguing. I was just commenting to my friend—oh, have you not met Miss Trevelyan? Then, pray, allow me to make her known to you."

Serena, who had been staring at her friend with wide-eyed wonder, turned to meet Rotterdam's amused glance. Humour warmed his green eyes and softened the harsh line of his lips. She gave him her hand and inclined her head politely.

"And are you bored as well, Miss Trevelyan?"

"No, my lord, but you must hold me excused. It is my first Season, you see," she explained with a smile. "Indeed, this is the first morning call I have paid."

"Then you have just arrived in Town?"

"Several weeks ago," she said, her dimple showing. "But my new dresses were not delivered until yesterday."

"I see," he said, barely concealing a grin. "And of course you could not be seen abroad with outdated fashions. It would certainly mark you a provincial."

"I suppose, but I dare say anyone would guess I am just up from the country in any case, though why that should be thought so undesirable, I am at a loss to know."

"Serena!" Cressy cried. "You must not say such things. Why, Lord Rotterdam will think you a...a dowd!"

"I doubt he will think of me at all," Serena replied, with a smile for the earl that clearly illustrated her lack of concern.

"You wrong me, Miss Trevelyan. I shall certainly think of you." His eyes darkened slightly as he looked down at her and allowed his gaze to travel slowly from the top of her dark curls to the tips of her kid boots peeping out from beneath her gown, and then back up to the slender column of her white throat.

"La, my lord, how you do take one up," Cressy said, tapping him lightly on his arm. "You must have a care or Miss Trevelyan shall be thinking you an accomplished flirt."

"I never indulge in light flirtation, Miss Appleby," he replied, his eyes still on Serena. "My intentions may not always be considered respectable, but they are nevertheless serious."

"Now I know how a poor field mouse feels when our cat toys with it," Serena said without thinking.

"I would not think of comparing you to a mouse, Miss Trevelyan," the earl said, ignoring Miss Appleby's gasp. "And can only hope you are not likening me to a cat."

Serena lowered her eyes, a smile playing about her lips.

"Egad, but you are! I am devastated!"

"Ah, but my cat is a very fine fellow," she said, peering up at him, her eyes brimming with laughter. "And an excellent hunter." Lord Rotterdam looked amused and Serena, seeing her mother and aunt approaching, added softly, "Of course, he always seeks out such helpless creatures."

"Rotterdam, a pleasure to see you again," Louisa said, coming up beside them and extending her hand.

"I see you have made the acquaintance of my niece, and judging by your expression, she has said something outrageous."

"Not at all," he said smoothly, bowing over her hand. "We were merely indulging in a game of cat and mouse."

Louisa looked puzzled, but he did not explain further and she quickly introduced him to Marjorie. There was a brief flicker of interest in his eyes, but it was gone in an instant as Mrs. Appleby and Lady Yarmouth joined them. He excused himself abruptly. "I see my sister wishes the pleasure of my company. Good day, ladies."

"Well," Louisa said, "he is ever the same. I declare he has not an ounce of civility."

"No, indeed, but he would be a wonderful catch for some young lady," Mrs. Appleby said, smiling fondly at her daughter. "They say he is one of the wealthiest men in all of England."

"Wealth is not everything," Marjorie said, staring after him.

"But, my dear Lady Trevelyan, he has the title, too. An earl is nothing to sneeze at!"

"Ha! Might as well wish for the moon," Lady Yarmouth declared. "Rotterdam is a hardened bachelor, and his reputation is such that I should not care to have him pay court to my daughter."

Cressida whispered to Serena, "Just as well. Her daughter has a squint and Rotterdam would not look twice at her."

THE DISTINGUISHING attention bestowed on Serena by Lord Rotterdam did not, of course, go unremarked. He rarely exchanged more than a word or two with any respectable lady, and to be seen conversing with Miss Trevelyan for a quarter-hour was sufficiently unusual to send the gossips scurrying about like a pack of hungry rats. The incident was elaborated, exaggerated, and embellished with all manner of unlikely detail.

By late evening, word had spread so rapidly through Town that nearly everyone who ventured out in polite Society was cognizant of the tale. Lord Lynton was one of the few gentlemen who remained in ignorance.

He had dined, quite privately, with Mrs. Tallant—a rare privilege, for usually the Brenermans were present. Angela Brenerman and her brother, George, were close friends of the widow's, and she had renewed the friendship on her return to England. This was unfortunate, in James's opinion, for he believed the couple's influence over her was responsible for the widow's occasional lapses from acceptable behaviour. When she was with them, she seemed a different person, more sophisticated, more cynical. He found Angela much too forward, and he deplored the familiar manner in which George Brenerman made himself at home in Mrs. Tallant's house. It sometimes seemed to James that the man was forever there, but tonight had been different.

Save for the presence of her maid, he'd had his lovely widow almost entirely to himself. She had been sweetness itself, and he had left feeling the same delicious enchantment that had first captivated him in Paris. Too elated to retire tamely to bed, James had given in to a strong impulse and ordered his groom to drive him to White's. He knew he could be certain of encountering one or two friends there with whom to share a drink and perhaps a game of cards or billiards, and he strolled into his club shortly after midnight.

He was hailed almost the moment he set foot in the card room. Lord Ormond, on the lookout for a fourth at whist, waved frantically from his table and called out, "Lynton, over here. Your luck is in—I need a partner. Will you join us?"

James pulled out a chair opposite the red-headed Ormond and grinned. "Depends upon the stakes. And where is Margate this evening? I thought he was your usual partner."

"Sloped off," Edward Kendrick informed him, shuffling a fresh deck of cards.

"That's what marriage does to a fellow," Gilbert Selwyn, the oldest of the foursome, added. "Barely midnight and he has to go home to his wife. Never thought I should live to see the day."

"Now, gentlemen, we must not be too hard on poor Harry. This marriage business is new to him," Lord Ormond said with a broad wink.

"Diamonds is trump," Kendrick announced, turning up the last card. "New or not, I dislike the way marriage has changed him. Disgraceful the way he trails about after his wife."

Silence reigned briefly while the trick was quickly played and Ormond pulled in the cards. "Speaking of marriage, is the wind blowing in your direction, Lynton? We've not seen much of you lately, either."

James took the trick with the king of diamonds and shrugged. He had gone to school with Ormond, and while he liked him well enough, he knew better than to confide anything in him that he didn't wish the whole Town to know. "It has its attractions. Who knows? I just may put my luck to the touch one of these days."

"Think it over carefully, my lord," Selwyn advised. "Marriage isn't something to go rushing into."

"How long have you been thinking it over, Gil? Five years? Ten?" Kendrick asked, chuckling.

"I've come close a time or two," he replied, unruffled. "Almost offered for Miss Grayson six years ago, and look how that turned out."

"I do not believe I know the lady," James said, playing the king of spades.

Selwyn trumped it with a diamond he'd held back. "See, lads, it pays not to rush your fences." He gathered in the cards and turned to James. "Miss Grayson was the toast of the Town when I first came to London. Never saw a prettier girl, either. Gad, but she was something," he said with a reminiscent air. Then he shook his head sadly. "Pity she took after her mama. Fat as a pig now. Breeding like one, too. Five babes she's got, and all of 'em girls!"

They all laughed at his ludicrous expression and Ormond clapped him on the shoulder. "My brother always said that nine times out of ten a young lady will turn out just like her mama, and Miss Grayson is an excellent case in point." He grinned at James across the table. "What about it, Lynton? How's your prospective mama-in-law look?"

James shook his head at such foolishness and took the deal, but he realized he knew very little about Mrs. Tallant's family and thought perhaps he should ask her where they were situated. Certainly he would have to make their acquaintance soon.

"Ha! There's Rotterdam," Kendrick whispered as the earl strode across the room. "Have you heard the latest on-dit?"

"That he gave his little actress her walking papers? You're a day late, Kendrick. I heard that at breakfast yesterday," Selwyn said.

"What?" Ormond cried. "Not the lovely Isabella? If that's true, I might have a touch at her myself."

"Take my advice and keep your distance. She'd cost you a bloody fortune!"

"I was *not* talking about Isabella," Kendrick said, careful to keep his voice low. "My sister told me Rotterdam was tipped a leveller this morning, and by a young chit just up from the country."

"Your sister is all abroad," Lord Ormond said with a chuckle. "All the world knows Rotterdam don't give the time of day to schoolroom misses."

"Well, he did to this one. My sister was there and she said he talked to the gel for above an hour."

"I don't believe it," Selwyn declared. "Not of Rotterdam! And where did your sister encounter him? Far as I know, he ain't in the habit of paying morning calls."

"He don't and that's a fact, but he does call on his sister now and again and that's where he was when he met this gel." Pleased with the astonishment he'd caused, Kendrick dealt the cards and turned up the queen of hearts. "There! That's an omen if ever I saw one."

"Well, don't stop now," Selwyn ordered. "Who is this lady capable of ensnaring Rotterdam?"

"Ain't acquainted with her myself. April said she's Lady Marcham's niece—a Miss Trevelyan."

James picked up his cards slowly. He had listened with half an ear and a good deal of amusement to his friends' talk. He didn't know Rotterdam, except by reputation, and had no interest in the man's flirts. But he was shaken by the mention of Serena's name. No, he told himself. It was not possible.

James misplayed a card, apologized, and glanced at Rotterdam across the room. Looking at him, it was easy to believe his reputation as a rake and a libertine. Whatever was Lady Marcham thinking of to bring Serena to his attention?

"I say, Lynton, that's the second time you've misplayed!"

"My apologies, Ormond. I fear I am more tired than I realized. Perhaps we should call it a night."

There were mumbled protests, but James was adamant. He took his leave, managing to respond to his friends' teasing without really being aware of what he was saying. His mind was fixed on Serena. He would have a word with Lady Marcham on the morrow, he decided. He should have called on her before now—had fully intended to—only Mrs. Tallant had required his escort to any number of engagements. With a groan he realized he'd promised to take the widow to view a balloon ascension the next day. Well, he'd send round a note crying off. Mrs. Tallant would understand. It was unfortunate, but he owed that much to Sir Laurence and Lady Trevelyan. They had always been most kind to him, and Serena was such an innocent. Almost against his will, he found his gaze drawn again to Rotterdam.

SATISFACTORY, most satisfactory, Eleazar thought, sitting in one of the comfortable armchairs and watching James as he prepared to take his leave. He'd had the devil's own time getting the boy out of the widow's clutches that evening. James could be stubborn when he chose, and the lady had been at her most charming. And despite what Cuthbert might say, one could hardly blame the lad. The widow was incredibly beautiful and

artfully skilled in the ways of love. She knew to a nice-
ness how to enslave a man. With some, it was revealing
gowns and passionate embraces. With others, like poor
Brenerman, she stroked their egos, lavish in her praise
of their manly attributes. With James, she preyed upon
his chivalry and innate kindness.

Well, two could play at that game. He had bided his
time, and had prompted Kendrick to mention the latest
gossip when Rotterdam had walked into the card room.
It was nearly sufficient in itself, but Eleazar had pricked
Jamie's conscience a bit. He'd reminded the lad he'd
neglected his childhood friend, and that she was straying into dangerous waters. It hadn't taken much to start
James worrying. A whispered reminder of the rake's
reputation had done the rest, and Eleazar had sat back
in his chair, well pleased.

He glanced at Rotterdam. The earl sat at his ease, a
bottle near his elbow and a large stack of chips before
him. He played carelessly, showing neither pleasure nor
concern. He was still immaculately attired, but his dark
curls had fallen over his brow and the green eyes held a
look of weariness. That, combined with the jagged scar
on his cheek, gave him just the sort of devilish good
looks to appeal to an innocent young girl like Serena.

He could prove useful, Eleazar thought. Just so long
as Serena did not become too infatuated. He'd have to
have a word with Cuthbert about it, but things were
looking promising. James, for once, was not thinking
of Mrs. Tallant.

CHAPTER FOUR

JAMES, fired with the zeal of good intentions and a nudge from Eleazar, arose early the following morning. He sat down to a light breakfast and, while he ate, composed a lengthy epistle to Mrs. Tallant. It was not an easy task, and the paper was soon barely legible with numerous lines crossed out and reworded, not to mention several traces of egg and strawberry preserves.

His valet, Cecil, watched him nervously. A gaunt man with a receding hairline, he thought perhaps he should retire and allow a younger man to attend his lordship. The past six months had been most difficult, particularly since the advent of Mrs. Tallant, and he'd developed a nervous tic in his right eye. But he was reluctant to give up the post and was as devoted to James as he had been to James's father before him. He sighed and reached for the coffee pot.

James pushed the dishes aside, accepted the fresh cup of coffee Cecil poured for him, and read the missive aloud. He changed another word or two, but on the whole was satisfied that he had adequately conveyed his remorse over the necessity of altering their plans, and that only the heavy onus of family duty kept him from her side.

Cecil, who had had enough to bear from the widow lady, felt a creeping sense of alarm at the mention of family and nearly dropped the dishes he was removing.

He swallowed hard, his Adam's apple bobbing. "Is Lady Lynton in town, my lord?"

"No, Mama's still at Wynyard Park," James murmured absently, his attention on penning a clean note.

"Thank heavens," Cecil muttered, and then hastily added, "Beggin' your pardon, sir, but I can't help thinking Lady Lynton would not approve of your rooms."

James glanced round the cluttered sitting-room. Several pairs of boots, riding crops, gloves and numerous newspapers were strewn about. His evening coat still lay across the chair where he had flung it the night before, and his beaver hat decorated a candle sconce. A half-dozen empty wine bottles reposed on the floor near the fireplace, along with a number of playing cards scattered about—the results of a late evening with one of his friends. Cecil did what he could, but it was getting beyond the older man, and since James rarely noticed the clutter, it mattered little. Except when Lady Lynton was in Town.

He grinned. "Mama would have a fit were she to see this, but you need not worry. When I mentioned family, I was referring to Serena."

"Miss Trevelyan, my lord?"

James nodded. "*She* is in Town, and what her mother can be thinking of, I am at a loss to know, but I feel it my duty to have a word with Lady Trevelyan. You know I have always regarded Serena as a sister."

"Is the young lady in some sort of trouble?" Cecil asked, recalling the engaging little imp who used to trail after his master and was forever in a scrape. He had helped Lord Lynton bail her out of trouble on more than one occasion.

"No—at least, not yet. But I happened to be at White's last night and you can imagine my utter amazement at hearing Serena's name coupled with that of a gentleman who is notorious for his scandalous affairs. I was never more shocked in my life."

"Quite understandable, my lord," Cecil agreed. His calm restored, he picked up a dish of bacon to remove it, but dropped it as suddenly, the china shattering as it crashed on the hardwood floor.

"What on earth?" James cried, springing up to avoid the flying shards of plate.

Cecil stood transfixed, a wavering finger pointing at the high-backed chair. "Stay back, my lord. There is some sort of creature beneath your coat. I saw it move! Do you think a—a rat has gotten in?"

James laughed, throwing back his head. "We shall not have any rats here, or mice either. Wait till you see what I found curled up on the doorstep." He strode towards the chair and, lifting off the coat, revealed a tiger-striped tom-cat, stretching languidly. The cat paused, regarding them with owlish green eyes.

James lifted it up by the scruff of its neck and carried the cat over to the table. "Here you go, Caesar. Breakfast is served." He sat it down amidst the broken china, and the cat, after stretching out his forelegs, sniffed daintily. A bit of bacon disappeared in a flash.

"A cat," Cecil murmured, watching as the sure-footed beast deftly extracted bits of bacon from between pieces of china.

"Not just any cat, my good man. He is obviously of royal descent. Only see how proudly he carries himself."

"But what are we to do with him?"

"Do? Why, nothing. The nice thing about owning a cat is that it requires little of you but a warm place to sleep. Just let him roam about the place and I dare say there won't be a mouse or rat left within miles."

"There will be if you feed him, my lord. I believe cats must be hungry before they hunt," Cecil said, still eying the creature warily. He'd seen the sharp claws flash out to snare a bit of meat.

"Oh well, a little treat now and then can't hurt—can it, Caesar, old boy?"

The cat, having picked out every piece of bacon, rubbed against his legs, signifying his approval with a loud purr.

James bent and obligingly scratched the animal's head. "He will be good company for you while I am out," he said, entirely missing the incredulous look on his valet's face.

"If you say so, my lord," Cecil agreed with resignation. Caesar was not the first animal his young master had rescued. At least, the cat was better than the mutt he'd picked up in Paris: a scrawny animal with his ribs all but showing and a limp in one leg. Covered with fleas, he'd been, too. It had fallen to Cecil to bathe the animal, and he'd been bitten twice for his pains. The mangy beast would likely still be with them if the widow lady hadn't taken an aversion to the animal. He smiled, remembering the scene Mrs. Tallant had created when she'd learned she was expected to ride in the same carriage with the mongrel. For once, his lordship had not been entirely enchanted with the lady.

JAMES, NEATLY ATTIRED in a well-fitting blue coat of Bath superfine from which Cecil had managed to brush all the cat hair, cream-coloured knee breeches, white stockings with blue clocks, and black shoes with a jewelled toe, at last set out for Manchester Square. The afternoon was sunny and he decided against taking his carriage. The square was not very far from his rooms and he could use the walk to order his thoughts.

A certain amount of diplomacy was called for in dealing with this matter. He could not very well tell either Lady Trevelyan or Lady Marcham that they had been remiss in chaperoning Serena. Such an implication on his part would no doubt be deemed an impertinence. No, he would have to behave as though this were just a neighbourly call on an old acquaintance. Then, in the course of the conversation, he could mention casually that he had heard Serena's name linked with that of Rotterdam, and he would express his surprise. Perhaps he might drop a hint that the gentleman's reputation was not all it should be.

He arrived on Lady Marcham's doorstep just as the clocks were chiming two, and used his cane to knock authoritatively on the door. It was opened almost immediately by a liveried footman, who stepped smartly back, allowing James entrance to the marbled foyer, where an imposing butler halted his progress.

"Good afternoon," James said, handing the man his card. "Please inform Lady Trevelyan that I would like a word with her."

The butler glanced from the card to Lord Lynton. They were of an equal height and he could not stare down his nose at the gentleman, but there was no doubting the frost in his voice when he replied nasally, "Her ladyship is not at home."

"Lady Marcham, then," James suggested, wondering if it was only his imagination that made him feel the butler somehow disapproved of him.

"Her ladyship is not at home, either," Pritchard repeated, making no move to take the proffered card.

"I see. And Miss Trevelyan?"

"Not at home, my lord."

"Do you perhaps know when the ladies are expected to return?" James asked, feeling unaccountably foolish.

"I am sure I could not say, my lord."

"I see. You will give Lady Trevelyan my card, then, and tell her, please, that I shall call again tomorrow and will hope for the pleasure of seeing her."

"If you insist, my lord," Pritchard said. He took the card James offered, and with an imperceptible nod to the footman, indicated that the door should be opened.

James left, wondering if he had a spot on his nose or if his cravat was stained. He glanced down at his coat. He was certain Cecil had removed all traces of cat hair, and his looking-glass had told him he appeared quite respectable. But he was convinced it was not merely his imagination; Lady Marcham's butler had definitely disapproved of him.

He strolled back to his rooms, his good mood evaporating. He had cancelled his engagement with Mrs. Tallant to no purpose. He should have guessed the ladies might be out and made some effort to learn Lady Marcham's day at home instead of giving in to a strong urge to visit her without delay.

Cecil opened the door to James, surprise showing on his thin features, and Caesar made a dive for the door, dashing past him and down the steps.

James, in his bemused state, hardly noticed. "Tell me, Cecil, is there something amiss with my attire?"

"My lord?"

"Is there anything about my dress to give you a dis-taste of me? I had the strangest experience at Lady Marcham's just now."

The valet obligingly studied him, but could find nothing to fault. Indeed, his lordship cut a handsome figure, and after a moment he shook his head.

James, standing before the looking-glass, had to, with all modesty, agree. Well, there was no accounting for it and no sense in worrying over it. It was possible the man merely had a sour countenance. He turned to his valet with a wry smile. "It is of no importance. Tell Paddy to have the carriage brought round. Perhaps I can still salvage something of the afternoon with Mrs. Tal-lant."

The widow had leased a house on Chesterfield Street. It was small and inexpensive, being just on the fringe of fashionable Mayfair, but within easy distance of all the shops and theatres. James arrived at half past two and was instantly admitted by the housekeeper. Feeling slightly better, he waited in the tiny sitting-room for Mrs. Tallant.

She came in a few moments later, a smile on her del-icate lips. "Why, James. What is this? I received your note this morning and was devastated. I was quite cer-tain I had not a prayer of seeing you today."

He bowed over her hand, drinking in the delicious scent of her. Everything about her was perfection, he thought as he straightened. It took him a moment to notice she had her hat on, and Mildred, her maid, was waiting by the door with her coat.

"I had thought to be obliged to spend the afternoon paying a duty call, but my plans were abruptly changed. I came round at once, but I apprehend you are on your way out?"

"Oh, if only I had known," Mrs. Tallant cried with a pretty pout, and peeped up at him beneath her heavy lashes. "I did so want to see the balloon ascension, James, and when your note came I was quite disappointed. Especially to think you would cast me aside without a second thought—"

"My dear Beryl, you know that could never be the case," he said fervently, taking her hand in his and gazing down into her limpid blue eyes. "It is only that Serena—Miss Trevelyan—has got herself into a bit of a spot and I felt I must have a word with her mother."

"I see," the widow murmured, and gently withdrew her hand. "It is Miss Trevelyan and not family obligations, as I thought, that drew you away."

"Serena has always been like a sister to me. I believe I explained that to you," he said with just the slightest touch of impatience.

"Oh, yes, of course. How delightful it must be for the child to have so many to look after her interests. You did say she was in Town with her mother? And staying with her aunt and uncle...and now she has you running to protect her." She turned her back to him, idly rearranging the flowers in the large vase before the window.

"I thought that you, of all people, would understand," he said.

"I?" she asked, turning to gaze up at him.

"You are very careful to safeguard your reputation," he said, gesturing to the woman waiting by the door. "I am never allowed to see you without your maid close by, and of course I respect you for that. You are aware of the irreparable damage rumours can do to a lady's reputation. But Serena is not so wise and has foolishly allowed her name to be linked with that of the worst sort of libertine! Her mother is new to Town and cannot know of the man's reputation. Surely, you can see it is my duty to have a word with her?''

"Yes, of course," she replied softly, and extended her hand. ''Come and sit beside me and tell me about this man who so worries you.'' When James hesitated, she smiled up at him. "You will forgive me, will you not, for being just the tiniest bit jealous of Miss Trevelyan? I envy her a little, having a family to look after her and someone so gallant as you to go rushing to her defence.''

"Now you are being absurd," he said, a warm smile erasing the harsh lines of his mouth. "As though someone as sophisticated and beautiful as yourself could ever be jealous of a little hoyden like Serena.''

Beryl Tallant lowered her eyes and pretended embarrassment, but she was well-pleased. This was more the passionate sort of declaration she was accustomed to from Lord Lynton. For a moment, she had been decidedly worried. He had sounded very nearly angry with her, and that would never do—not if she were to bring him to the point where he would disregard his mother's wishes and offer her marriage.

"You exaggerate, but thank you, James. Now, tell me. What have you heard of Miss Trevelyan to alarm you?''

"Her name was coupled with that of Lord Rotterdam. I doubt if you know the gentleman, but his reputation is such that, well, it could do Serena a great deal of harm.''

Mrs. Tallant paled slightly, but James was looking down at his hands and did not notice. Her hands trembled, so she clasped them tightly and took a deep breath while James haltingly told her of what he'd heard at

White's the evening before. By the time he had done, she had regained a measure of composure and was able to smile at him.

"Surely you are making too much of this. I know Lord Rotterdam has a scandalous reputation, but I have never heard it said that he dallies with young girls."

"I hope you are correct, but you do understand why I must have a word with Lady Trevelyan, do you not? Unfortunately, she was not at home today, and I had to leave word I would call again tomorrow."

"Of course I do, but—oh dear, must it be tomorrow? Have you forgotten that we are promised to the Brenermans? Everything is all arranged, and I was so looking forward to our little expedition."

"As was I, but surely we can postpone it?" James suggested, not entirely displeased, for spending an entire day in George Brenerman's company was not his notion of enjoyment.

"I do not see how. Angela would be terribly disappointed were I to cry off now. You must know she has gone to a great deal of trouble...but of course, you must do as you think best."

Another gentleman might have recognized the anger beneath those words and immediately changed his own plans. James saw only her generosity and understanding, and proposed instead that they attend the theatre on her return. "Then you may tell me all about it," he added.

The knocker sounded before she could answer, and she rose abruptly. "I fear you must excuse me now, James. That will be Captain Stewart, who has most kindly offered to escort me to see the balloon ascension in your stead." She saw his look of consternation and gave him her hand. "I would so much rather it was you, but when I mentioned how disappointed I was, Patrick offered.'' She shrugged. ''What could I say? But you need not worry, my dear, we shall be well chaperoned. George and Angela are going with us.''

''I see,'' James replied stiffly as he rose. ''I shall bid you good-day, then.''

Captain Stewart, looking extremely smart in his scarlet regimentals, was admitted to the room just as James was leaving. There was an awkward moment at the door, and the gentlemen nodded politely to each other. They had met on several occasions, but James was not well acquainted with the older man and at the moment wished him to the devil.

Beryl Tallant watched him leave, a satisfied smile on her pretty lips.

SERENA RETURNED home that same afternoon anxious to tell Annie about the amusing gentleman she had met at Lady Saltwood's and the funny twin sisters who had the diverting habit of finishing each other's sentences. She put off her bonnet and gloves and rang for her maid, but it was several minutes before the girl appeared.

Serena, seated at her dressing-table, turned excitedly when she heard the door open. ''Oh, Annie, I have so much to tell you!''

''And I have news for you, miss,'' the maid replied with a smile. She crossed the room and directed Serena to turn her head so she might begin to remove the pins from her hair. ''Your young gentleman was here this afternoon.''

''Jamie?'' Serena cried, twisting round in her chair. ''Annie, was he truly here? What did he say? Is he coming back?''

Annie nodded tiredly and barely managed to smother a yawn before she replied, "Pritchard said he left word for Lady Trevelyan that he will call again tomorrow."

"Did you see him, Annie? Is he not handsome? Oh, how I wish I had been at home."

"Just as well you were not, miss. Do him a bit of good to find you're not sitting here just waiting on his pleasure. Now, let me brush your hair out. Lady Marcham said as how you should rest a bit before dinner."

Serena laughed. "I could never rest now—I am far too excited. What did you think of him, Annie? Is he not wonderful?"

"I was in the kitchen and never saw him, miss. It was Thomas, the second footman, who told me. He was in the hall with Pritchard when Lord Lynton called, but he did say your young gentleman seemed a bit disappointed to find you not at home."

She didn't add that Thomas had told her old Pritchard had been as starched up with the young lord as he dared. The staff, with the sole exception of Mrs. Moppit, had taken to Miss Serena and did not look kindly on the young man who had caused her to cry her eyes out when she thought no one was about.

"I must go down and speak to Mama and Aunt Louisa at once," Serena declared. "They have plans for tomorrow, but I know Mama will understand that I must be here when Jamie comes back."

"It would not hurt him to find you absent, miss," Annie suggested, with no real hope of being attended to. Not when Serena's face glowed at the mere thought of seeing Lord Lynton. She prevailed on her charge to at least allow her to brush her hair out, but it was not an

easy task with Serena squirming in her chair and anxious to be belowstairs.

"Thank you, Annie," Serena said when at last she
was done, and she squeezed the maid's hand. "I shall
be back in a few minutes."

"Yes, miss," the maid murmured, sinking wearily
down on the bed as soon as the door closed behind Serena. She only needed to rest for a few moments, she
thought, and closed her eyes.

Serena fairly skipped down the stairs, but mindful of
her mother's dictum on the proper way for a young lady
to enter a room, she paused outside the sitting-room.
She smoothed the skirt of her muslin dress, brushed the
long curls back off her shoulder and took a deep breath.
Then, softly, she opened the door.

Louisa and Marjorie were seated together on the love-
seat in front of the fireplace, deep in conversation.
Neither heard the door open. Serena was about to in-
terrupt when she heard Jamie's name mentioned.

"Perhaps I should forbid Serena to see James,"
Marjorie was saying doubtfully.

"I do not believe it would answer," Louisa replied.
"I recall when Papa ordered you not to see Laurence.
If anything, it made you all the more obstinate!"

"That was entirely different. Laurence and I were in
love and he had already offered for me. James...James
has been like a son to us. He cares for Serena, but as he
would for a younger sister." Marjorie shook her head
distractedly. "I fear there can be nothing for Serena but
heartbreak if she continues with this mad obsession."

"Perhaps, but if you deny her a chance with young
Lynton, how do you suppose she will feel when he
eventually weds another? She would surely blame you,
Marjorie, and it would always stand between you. If

you are indeed asking my advice, I think you must allow Serena her heartache. However much you love her, you cannot protect her forever.''

"Louisa, she is still so young!"

"She is old enough to marry, my dear, and old enough to have fallen in love with Lynton.''

"Nonsense! She is still a child and knows only this blind adoration for a boy she has toddled after since she was old enough to walk. That is not love.''

Louisa reached over and patted her sister's hand. "You must do as you think best, but I pray you will not discount Serena's feelings. You fell in love with Laurence at first sight, but that is not to say a young girl cannot love a gentleman she has known all her life just as deeply. Sometimes I think when it takes one very young like that, it must be the hardest of all to bear.''

There was a poignant note in her sister's voice, and Marjorie looked at her curiously. "You sound as if—''

"We are not discussing me,'' Louisa interrupted, and reached for the teapot to refill their cups. "I am only saying that you should not entirely disregard the way Serena feels.''

"Oh, Lord, I do wish Laurence were here,'' Marjorie murmured. She glanced round, thinking she heard the door, but there was no one there.

Serena leaned against the closed door, feeling faint. Mama could not seriously be thinking of forbidding her to see Jamie. The thought was unbearable. Why, one might as well order her not to breathe! She'd known her mother did not understand her devotion to Jamie. Indeed, the purpose of their journey to London was to introduce Serena to other eligible young gentlemen, and Serena had understood that. But deep in her heart she had also known that she would see Jamie again in London, and it was the only reason she had agreed to come. Of course, she had not confided that to Mama. She'd long ago given up trying to convince Mama that there was no one else for her but Jamie.

Jamie. Had she only imagined he returned her love? Was that possible when she was so certain in her heart that they were meant for each other?

"Is there something I can help you with, miss?"

Startled, Serena looked up to find Mrs. Moppit watching her with narrowed, disapproving eyes. She flushed guiltily and shook her head.

"Very well, miss, but I am sure her ladyship would prefer you not to linger in the hall."

"I was about to speak with my mother only... only I find I forgot my handkerchief."

"Of course, miss," the housekeeper agreed, her lips twisting in a knowing smile.

Without another word, Serena lifted her chin and brushed past her. She could feel the woman's eyes on her as she started up the stairs and had to resist a strong urge to run. She turned at the landing and glanced down. Mrs. Moppit, her arms folded across her chest, was standing at the foot of the steps, staring up at her. Serena shivered and quickly crossed the hall.

"Annie—" she began as she stepped into her room, but bit off her words. Her maid was curled up at the foot of the bed, and judging from the light snores, sound asleep. Serena watched her for a moment, thinking the poor girl must be exhausted. There were dark smudges beneath her eyes and, if it were possible, Annie looked even thinner than she had a few weeks ago. Serena quietly removed a quilt from the storage chest and gently spread it over her, then retreated to the window-seat.

She tucked her feet beneath her on the padded cushion and leaned against the wall. Her stay in London was not turning out as she had expected, she thought, idly watching the passing carriages. She had been so certain that everything here would be wonderful—and that all she needed in the world was to see Jamie again. But her meeting with him had been filled with disappointment. Tears crept into her eyes as she considered her mother's words. Was it possible? Had she been blind to Jamie's true feelings?

She recalled the last time she had seen him at home. Jamie had ridden out with her, and when they had reached the river, they had tied the horses to a shrub and walked along the bank. Serena had sensed at once that something was terribly wrong and had listened in stunned silence when Jamie told her he was going abroad.

She had felt as though the earth was tilting beneath her feet, and it was only Jamie's strong arm about her that prevented her from stumbling. Alarmed by her pale colour, he had carried her tenderly to the base of an old oak tree, and insisted she sit there and rest.

Serena had stared at him, trying to memorize the lines of his face, not even realizing her eyes were filling with tears.

"What is this?" Jamie murmured, and, withdrawing his handkerchief, dabbed at the teardrops on her cheek. "It's not as though I am going away forever. There is no reason for tears."

"Oh, Jamie, you will come back?" Serena pleaded, catching at his hand and holding it to her cheek.

"Of course I shall, you goose. Wynyard is my home."

"I know, but Jamie, I am so afraid. I feel as though I am losing you. You will forget all about me," she said, choking back a sob.

"Impossible, imp," he said, flicking the tip of her nose with his finger. "I promise you I will come back—that is, if you promise to wait for me," he added with a grin, hoping to tease her into better spirits.

"I will always wait for you," she swore with a solemnity that shook him.

"Good Lord, Serena! You are too young to know what you are saying. Why, in another year or two you will laugh at this day and wonder how you ever could have been so foolish."

She shook her head, biting her lip, and her wide brown eyes still glistened with tears.

Jamie, unable to bear the sadness expressed there, turned away and idly plucked some flowering rush growing along the bank. "Serena, I have no choice but to go, though if it makes you feel better, I promise you I shall return. And I promise you nothing could ever make me forget you. Will you believe that?"

She nodded, her throat too tight to speak.

Jamie had twisted a stem of a flower into a semblance of a ring, and he took Serena's hand and slipped it over her finger. "There! Consider that a pledge."

The flower ring had long since wilted, but Serena still had it pressed between the pages of her Bible. From that day until now, she had regarded herself as promised to Jamie. Had she been wrong? Was the ring just a token to soothe her hurt feelings? Did Jamie, like her mother, regard her love as nothing more than a childish obsession?

The idea was frightening. Small tendrils of fear snaked through her, gripping her so strongly that for a moment her heart stopped beating and she could not think clearly. Then she heard the voice.

Jamie loves you. He is confused, but you must have faith in him. Don't give up. Remember, he loves you.

The calm, reassuring power of the words eased the tightness in her chest. A soft tap on the door brought her to her feet, and she wiped at her eyes as she swiftly crossed the room. She opened the door an inch or so and was relieved to see one of the parlour-maids. "Yes, Etta?"

"Mrs. Moppit sent me up, miss. She said Annie is wanted in the kitchen if you don't need her up here no more."

"Tell Mrs. Moppit that Annie is arranging my hair in a new style and I shall require her services until dinner."

Etta's eyes grew round, and she blinked at Serena, whose long brown hair was still cascading down her back exactly as it had been that morning. "Yes, miss," she said after a pause, and then smiled crookedly. "I'll tell her, miss."

"Thank you, Etta," Serena said softly, and gently shut the door.

Their conversation had disturbed Annie. She opened her eyes and struggled up. It took her a moment to realize where she was, and then she hastily scrambled off the bed. "Miss Serena! I never meant to—"

"It's quite all right, Annie. It is obvious you were exhausted. Have you been ill?"

The girl hung her head. "No, miss. I'll be fine. I'm only a bit tired, is all."

"Are you in some sort of trouble, Annie?" Serena asked gently. "I can see that you have lost weight, and I should have noticed before that you are terribly pale."

"It's nothing, miss."

"Look at me, Annie," Serena demanded. "I cannot help you if you will not confide in me. Is it Mrs. Moppit? Is she ill-treating you?"

Tears formed in the maid's eyes and she sniffed. "She didn't like it that I went to the tooth-puller. She says I must make up for the time I missed and she's been givin' me extra chores. I don't get but two or three hours' sleep a night."

"I see. Well, we shall put a stop to that at once!"

"Oh, miss, please don't say nothin'," Annie begged. "It would only make things worse. There ain't nothin' you can do."

"Papa would say that people who sit about bemoaning their fate and doing nothing to help themselves deserve what they get. I'm glad you made me remember that, Annie," Serena said with a strange smile. "I was almost ready to give up everything most dear to me."

"I don't understand, miss," Annie said with a bemused look.

"It does not matter," Serena said, crossing the room to her dressing-table. "Just remember that nothing is ever hopeless, not if you are determined to do something about it. Now, come and help me, Annie. I dislike the way my hair is arranged. I want something very modish. Perhaps we should cut it?"

"Oh no, miss. It looks very sweet."

"But I have no wish to look sweet. I want to look beautiful, Annie and... and sophisticated! Perhaps some curls about my brow?" she suggested, recalling Mrs. Tallant's elegant coiffure.

Annie lifted a handful of Serena's dark hair. "It would be a shame to cut it, miss." She sniffed again, but her tears were drying and there was a sparkle of interest in her eyes as she considered the problem. She picked up the brush and separated several strands. "I could put it all up in a topknot with a braid round it, miss. It would look rather like a crown."

Serena agreed to allow her to try and sat quietly while her maid worked. Though her gaze was on the looking-glass in front of her, she hardly noticed what Annie was doing. Her thoughts were all of Jamie. If her mother was correct and Jamie thought of her as a little sister, then she would have to contrive to make him see her in a new manner, to make him realize he loved her as much as she loved him.

She was still wrestling with ideas of how that might be accomplished when Annie stepped back. "There, miss," she said with a pleased smile.

Serena studied her reflection. Certainly she looked different. It was odd seeing her hair done up so smoothly without any trace of curls or ribbons to adorn it. "It looks rather plain," she said hesitantly, and continued to study her image. "But I believe I like it, Annie. It is very...elegant."

"It becomes you, miss," her maid agreed with a trace of pride.

Serena rose. "We shall put it to the test and see what Mama and Aunt Louisa think. Heavens, it is quite late. Hurry, Annie, and help me change for dinner."

There was barely time for Serena to change her dress, but with Annie's help she was ready just as the clock chimed seven. She paused at the door and looked back at her maid, already busily tidying the room. "Annie," she called, a mischievous light in her eyes. "I am finding it very difficult to sleep at night. Doubtless it is all the strange noises of London that keep me awake, but I believe I should feel safer if you would not object to sleeping in my room. I shall ask my aunt to have a trundle-bed moved in here.''

''Mrs. Moppit won't allow it, miss,'' Annie warned, even while hope warmed her eyes.

''We shall see,'' Serena said.

CUTHBERT, trailing her out of the room, halted at the top of the stairs and sank wearily down to rest for a moment. It had been touch-and-go there for a while. He had never felt so much nervous agitation—no, not even in the days when he was leading a cavalry charge. This guardian business was worse than any battle he'd ever fought. Heaven help her, he prayed. Serena's happiness was such a fragile thing to have in his hands, and he feared he wasn't wise enough to guide her.

And Eleazar was of little help. Him with his code of conduct. Can't do this, can't do that. How in Heaven's name were they supposed to accomplish anything hemmed in by rules and regulations as they were? He did give Eleazar credit for getting Jamie to call. That, at least, was a start, but more was needed if they were to see this thing through—more than the rules allowed. And if it cost him his place in Heaven, so be it.

He felt a cold draught on his back and quickly moved aside as Mrs. Moppit swept down the hall. That was another thing: here was this evil woman, and he wasn't permitted to so much as give her a gentle nudge down the stairs. ''Against regulations,'' Eleazar would say. Cuthbert rose and drifted down the steps behind Serena, keeping a close eye on her. He'd abide by the book for now, but if the woman tried to do anything to harm the girl, he'd tell Eleazar what he could do with his rules!

CHAPTER FIVE

SERENA'S MIND was whirling as she stepped from her room. There was much to think about, particularly in regard to Jamie, but first Annie's problem needed to be addressed. Serena felt responsible for the girl's miserable position in the household and knew her papa would agree it was her duty to see to her maid's well-being, even if he did not entirely condone her methods.

The proper, logical thing to do, of course, would be to confide in Aunt Louisa. She ought to simply tell her that Mrs. Moppit was treating Annie most unfairly and leave her aunt to deal with the housekeeper. But Serena suspected her aunt was too much in fear of the woman to risk offending her, and if she spoke to Mrs. Moppit at all, she would only in putting the housekeeper's back up and making the situation far worse for Annie.

Knowing there was only one person capable of circumventing Mrs. Moppit, Serena hurried down the steps, across the hall to the library, and swiftly lifted her hand, tapping lightly on the door.

Her uncle's deep voice bade her enter and she slipped in, carefully shutting the door behind her. He was seated at a large oak desk covered with various papers and journals, and the pungent aroma of his cigar filled the air. Sylvester was expecting a footman, come to summon him to the drawing-room, and it was a moment before he looked up.

He smiled broadly then, seeing it was Serena, and stood up. "Well, puss, you are looking exceptionally lovely. Come give your old uncle a kiss."

Serena crossed the room and stood on tiptoe to plant a chaste salute on the leathery cheek. "Good evening, sir. I wondered if I might have a word with you before dinner."

"Of course, of course. Sit down, my dear, and tell me what I can do for you. A new dress, a hat? Run through your pin-money, have you?"

Serena shook her head, smiling at him. "You must know I have not, when you and my aunt have been so exceedingly generous. Indeed, sir, Mama fears I am in danger of becoming spoiled."

"Nonsense. A girl only makes her bow to Society once, and truth be told, it is I who am indebted to you. Louisa is enjoying herself immensely. Why, she bent my ear for near to an hour last evening with the details of your Court dress."

"It is beautiful," Serena said, "and I am at a loss how to thank you. It makes it particularly awkward to—to ask you . . ."

"What is it, child? Come, there's no need to be shy with me."

Serena ducked her head, a blush stealing into her cheeks. Her uncle was everything that was kind and she hated deceiving him. Twisting her hands in her lap, she looked up beseechingly. "I am afraid you will think me vastly foolish, sir, and I loathe the idea of being a troublesome guest. Papa says there is nothing worse than a visitor who throws the entire household into disorder, so if it would be a great deal of bother, you must not hesitate to say so. I dare say I shall grow accustomed to all the strange noises."

"Strange noises? I fear I am dense this evening," Sylvester murmured. "Whatever are you talking of, my dear?"

"Why, all the commotion in the streets at night," Serena replied, gesturing towards the windows. "It is foolish to be alarmed, I suppose, but I wondered if my maid might be permitted to sleep in my room? If you would not dislike the notion, I could ask the house-keeper to move a trundle-bed into my chamber for her. I think I should sleep much better with Annie there, and then she would be on hand to help me whenever I wished."

"Well, of course, if that is what you desire," her uncle replied, looking somewhat confused. "But if you are not sleeping well, my dear, you should have mentioned it to your aunt."

Serena nodded, a chastened look in her brown eyes. "I meant to do so, but Aunt Louisa would be distressed to think I was not comfortable, and I know she would not like to speak to Mrs. Moppit about it."

"Who," Sylvester said slowly, "is Mrs. Moppit?"

"Why, your housekeeper, sir. My aunt told me you are well-pleased because Mrs. Moppit runs your home precisely as you desire, and good housekeepers are extremely hard to find in London." Serena paused, trying to judge his reaction before adding with a light laugh, "I know it must seem absurd, but I believe my aunt is almost afraid of the woman."

"What balderdash," Sylvester muttered, his good humour rapidly disappearing. "If Louisa is not pleased with her housekeeper, she has only to discharge her.

You are letting your imagination run away with you, child.''

"Perhaps," Serena agreed, shrugging prettily. "I know *you* would never be intimidated by Mrs. Moppit, but I own she frightens me terribly, and I would not dare approach her without your express permission." She rose from her chair and smiled ruefully. "Pray, forgive me, Uncle. It was thoughtless of me to come to you. Papa would say I am repaying your generosity with ingratitude, complaining of such a trifling disturbance."

"Sit down, Serena," he ordered, and when she had seated herself again, he said, "Your consideration for your aunt does you credit, even if it is misplaced." He pulled the bell rope behind the desk, and added, "However, the problem is easily resolved."

A discreet scratch on the door signalled the arrival of the footman, and Sylvester directed the man to summon the housekeeper.

Serena rose again. "Perhaps I should—"

"Please remain, my dear. I should like you to see for yourself that there is nothing to fear from servants. A firm hand is all that is needed."

Serena sat down, hoping she appeared more composed than she felt. A confrontation with Mrs. Moppit was the last thing she desired, but it appeared inevitable.

Sylvester saw her discomfort and tried to put her at ease, rambling on about the difficulties of adjusting to life in London, where the streets were rarely quiet and the sound of carriages could be heard till the small hours of the morning. "Not to mention the cries of those idiotic watchmen. Bumbling incompetents, the lot of them, and I intend to bring it to the attention of the

House of Lords. I am glad you put me in mind of it, child.''

Serena listened with a flattering air of rapt attention. ''I was certain you would understand, Uncle, though I am indeed sorry to put you to so much trouble. But I confess it would be a relief to know that Annie is in the room with me at night.''

Her uncle was not unmoved by the anxiety in her eyes—though he thought her concern foolish—and he spoke brusquely to the housekeeper when she stepped into the room a moment later.

''There is to be a change or two, Mrs. Moppit,'' he began jovially. ''My little niece is having a bit of a problem sleeping at night. Would you see a trundle-bed is moved into her room?''

''A trundle-bed, my lord?'' the woman repeated incredulously, shooting a dark glare at Serena.

Sylvester missed it, having turned his head to smile at his niece in a fond manner. ''Yes, at once. We cannot have the child making her come-out with shadows beneath her eyes,'' he said with a chuckle. ''That maid—Annie? Annie shall sleep there.''

''Really, my lord, Annie is needed—''

Sylvester glanced up at the housekeeper, a look of astonishment in his eyes. ''Surely you are not questioning my orders, Mrs. Moppit?''

''No, my lord. Of course not, my lord. 'Tis only, with guests in the house we are short-staffed and the girl is needed in the kitchen.''

''You have my leave to engage another girl. See to it that my wishes are carried out at once. That is all.''

The housekeeper curtsied and swiftly left the room, but not before Serena had seen the look of fury in her eyes. She knew she had been wise to bring her request to her uncle.

"There, that was not so difficult, was it?" Sylvester said, rising and coming round the desk to give Serena his arm. "And now, I believe we had best join the ladies."

Serena agreed and strolled arm in arm with him to the drawing-room. She listened to her uncle's conversation with the appearance of attentiveness, but her mind was already considering her next problem: Jamie's visit.

Her mother and aunt were seated together on the sofa that faced away from the door. Sylvester spoke as they entered. "Well, now, I call this pleasant, finding two of the loveliest ladies in London waiting for me. And I've brought another to join you."

Marjorie turned slightly to welcome them, but the ready smile died on her lips. "Serena! Whatever have you done to your hair?"

"Do you not care for it, Mama? I thought perhaps a new style..."

"It looks entirely charming, dear," Louisa said, coming to her niece's rescue. Patting the seat beside her, she added, "Come and sit next to me."

"Thought there was something different about you," Sylvester said, watching Serena gracefully cross the room. "Very pretty."

"I fear I cannot agree," Marjorie said, studying her daughter. "However stylish, it makes you appear much older than your years and is far too severe a coiffure for a girl of your age."

"Now, Marjorie, you sound just like Mama did when *we* first put our hair up," Louisa said, patting her sister's hand. "I suppose all mothers are the same and loathe seeing their little girls change into young ladies.

Do you remember how Mama cried the first time she saw you in a ball dress? It was the palest of blues with layers and layers of netting, and Nanna said you were the loveliest thing she'd ever seen. You quite put *my* nose out of joint!''

Marjorie smiled at her sister's teasing, but her eyes were still on Serena. "There can be no comparison, Louisa. You and I looked like all the other young girls, and as I recall, we were a bundle of nerves. Serena looks—well, so much older."

"All the better if she does, if you ask me," Sylvester said, chuckling. "Take my word for it—nothing worse for a young gentleman than to walk into a room full of young ladies all looking just like peas in a pod. Not a thing to distinguish one from the other, if you know what I mean. Now, our little Serena here will make an impression. All the young bucks will remember her."

Marjorie was not at all certain she wished her daughter to be singled out in such a manner, but she glanced again at Serena and reluctantly owned the style did flatter her. "Only it is very misleading," she added with a faint smile. "Judging by appearances, one would expect a very refined young lady. You will have to cultivate a new manner."

"I shall try, Mama," Serena promised, her dimple peeping out and her eyes alight with amusement.

It quite destroyed her air of sophistication and restored her once again to the rank of a schoolroom miss, much to Marjorie's relief, but there was no time to say anything more. Pritchard tapped on the door and announced dinner was served. Sylvester gallantly gave his arm to his sister-in-law, and Louisa followed them out with her arm linked through Serena's.

"I believe once your mama becomes accustomed to your new coiffure, she will like it very well. It is really most becoming."

"Thank you," Serena replied, grateful for the small kindness and praying she would retain her aunt's good opinion when that lady learned of the encounter with Mrs. Moppit.

The moment was not long in coming. The first course had just been served when Sylvester mentioned the matter. He passed it off as an amusing anecdote, teasing Serena over her fears, both of the housekeeper and the strange noises she heard at night.

Louisa laughed, as her husband expected her to do, but had his attention not been focused on his soup, he would have observed the way the colour faded from her face. Marjorie, hiding her surprise that her daughter had trouble sleeping, eyed Serena speculatively. She was quite certain her child had another reason for her actions, but decided the subject would best be broached in private.

Louisa, aware of the tension in the air, made haste to change the course of conversation, and the rest of the dinner passed in relative peace. Serena was careful to say nothing to which anyone could possibly take exception, and gave every appearance of being a docile young lady listening respectfully to her elders discuss the notable personages presently in Town.

It was not until the ladies left Sylvester to his cigars and port, and were comfortably settled in the drawing-room, that Serena dared to mention Jamie's call. She waited until her mother and aunt were seated on the sofa and then casually took the gilded chair in front of the spinet. Pretending an unconcern she was far from feeling, Serena leafed through the sheets of music.

After a moment, she glanced over her shoulder, and though her smile was composed, her heart was racing wildly. She prayed her voice would not betray her agitation. "Mama, did Pritchard tell you Jamie called today? I have been expecting him, of course, but is it not just like him to choose a time when we were otherwise engaged?" She turned back to the music and idly struck a few chords.

Marjorie looked helplessly at her sister, but Louisa merely shrugged. It was not her decision to make.

"He is coming back tomorrow," Serena added, and looked over her shoulder again at her mother. "Would it be unforgivable to cry off from Mrs. Trenton's? I should dearly love to see Jamie and hear all his news. But, if you dislike the notion, perhaps we could invite him to dine with us later in the week."

Marjorie sighed, wishing once more that Laurence was there to guide her, for she did not at all know what was best to do. Serena appeared untroubled, her dark, smooth head bent over the sheet music and her delicate hands moving gracefully over the ivory keys. She did not seem in the least excited at the thought of seeing James—and that in itself was reason for unease.

Serena finished the tune with a flourish and twisted round to face her mother with a wistful smile. "That is one of Papa's favourite pieces. Do you remember it, Mama? I vow it makes me feel almost homesick. It would be nice to visit with Jamie tomorrow. Seeing someone from home would not make Malmesbury seem so far away."

"Would it not? I am surprised, considering James has not been near the place for above two years," her mother answered a trifle tartly.

Serena giggled. "You are right, Mama. More than likely, he will wish to hear all our news and Aunt Louisa would be bored to tears. Shall I just leave him a note?"

"Do not consider me, child," Louisa said, looking up from her needlepoint. "If you wish to remain at home, I shall call on Mrs. Trenton myself and extend your apologies."

Marjorie did not like it. She had been certain Serena would be thrilled to learn James had called, and had anticipated heart-wringing pleas from her daughter to remain at home for his visit. Serena's apparent lack of concern should have been reassuring, but it only served to convince Marjorie that her child was up to mischief. Still, there appeared no hope of avoiding James altogether and little to be gained by delaying the inevitable.

"I suppose it would only be civil to receive his call. Louisa, are you certain Mrs. Trenton will not be offended?"

"Quite. You need not worry. I shall explain the circumstances."

Serena, hiding her gleeful smile, turned back to the spinet. She would have liked to have expressed her soaring spirits with a rousing concerto, but mindful of her mother's watchful eyes, she chose a sweet melody that would not intrude overly much on the conversation. When she finally rejoined the ladies, she was careful not to mention Jamie, though she thought of nothing else.

"HE'S HERE, miss," Annie said from her post at the window, watching the handsome young man step down from his carriage.

Serena fairly danced across the room and was in time to catch a glimpse of Jamie before he disappeared from view. "Oh, he looks splendid, does he not, Annie?"

Her maid nodded. It was difficult to fault the gentleman. He wore a deep claret cutaway coat over a patterned waistcoat and buff pantaloons. Wellington boots of black calfskin fitted his legs as snugly as the coat fitted his wide shoulders. His slender build suited the style admirably, and Annie could see why her mistress was so taken with the gentleman. "Very handsome, miss."

Serena, hurrying back to stand before the looking-glass, barely heard her. She was having second thoughts over her attire and her new hairstyle. She had chosen one of her new morning dresses—a pretty shade of jonquil puffed at the shoulders and with long sleeves tapering to a point above her wrists. Annie assured her it set off her dark hair to perfection.

"Perhaps I should let my hair down? Jamie has always admired my curls," she confided with a nervous laugh. "He might not recognize me! Oh, dear. Annie, maybe the blue walking dress would be—"

"You look lovely, miss, and you haven't time to change now. Go on now with you or your gentleman will be thinking you abandoned him."

Serena had to smile at such a notion, but she took a deep breath, straightened her shoulders and murmured a prayer before leaving the room. *Jamie was waiting for her.* The thought filled Serena with an unbearable excitement, and it was all she could do not to fly down the stairs and hurl herself into his arms. She held tightly to the curving mahogany banister, using it to slow her steps while telling herself she must not appear too eager to see her beloved again.

She was almost undone when she heard his voice, the melodious sounds floating out to her from the drawing-room. She paused for a moment, closing her eyes to savour the deep richness of it, and thought no one had a voice quite as lovely as Jamie's.

"Are you ill, Miss Trevelyan?"

The rough words of Mrs. Moppit startled her, and Serena blushed at being caught day-dreaming. "I am fine, thank you."

"If you say so, miss," the housekeeper replied. She crossed her beefy arms and remained standing near the door.

Serena swept past her, repressing a shiver at the dislike in the woman's eyes, and stepped into the drawing-room. Mrs. Moppit was forgotten in the next instant. She saw Jamie across the room, sitting next to her mother, his handsome blond head bent as he listened attentively.

James looked up a second later and blinked as he rose fluidly to his feet. "Serena?"

"Good day, Jamie," she said, crossing the room and extending one delicate hand in greeting as she had seen her aunt do. "How delightful to see you again."

"And you, too," he replied, taking her hand and executing a neat bow. His blue eyes held a puzzled look as he studied her. "I vow I scarcely recognize you, Serena. You look very pretty in your Town dress."

"Do I?" she asked, hating to let go of his hand. She wondered he could not feel the tingle that ran through her at his touch.

"Very," he replied with a warm smile. "Though I must confess, I think I rather miss the little ragamuffin who used to dog my footsteps."

"Nothing remains the same," Lady Trevelyan said, and indicated Serena should take the place beside her. "I was just speaking to James of some of the changes under way at Wynyard Park and how surprised I was to learn he was in Town." She turned to him again. "I rather thought you would wish to be there to oversee the renovations."

"Oh, Mother has it well in hand. I had a letter from her a few days ago and she writes everything is progressing smoothly."

"You must send her my regards when next you write. I gather she is fixed at Wynyard for some time, then?"

"At least a month or two, but she plans to visit my sister at Norwich as soon as it may be arranged," he said, and added with a confiding smile, "Olivia has sent word that she hopes to announce a happy event near Christmas, and of course wishes to have her mother near."

"Very understandable," Marjorie murmured with a pointed glance at Serena. It really was not a suitable conversation for her ears.

James, however, was oblivious to the delicate hint. He had always spoken freely before Serena and he continued blithely, "You may imagine how distracted Mama is. She can barely wait to shake the dust of Malmesbury from her shoes, and I expect I shall have to cut the Season short here and return home to oversee the renovations myself."

"But don't you *want* to go home, Jamie?" Serena asked. Next to Jamie and her family, she loved Malmesbury more than anything in the world. The thought of willingly staying away for years was as incomprehensible to her as the sun failing to rise.

"Of course I do," he said with a teasing grin. "But Town life has its attractions, too. I wager a few more weeks in London will find you less than eager to return home." He hesitated and then added, "In fact, I hear you have already made a conquest."

Marjorie's hands stilled on the needlepoint she held in her lap, and she lifted her brows. "Indeed?"

He laughed, trying to make light of the matter. "Yes, you can only imagine my surprise to hear at my club that Serena had quite captivated the Earl of Rotterdam. It was said he spoke with her at great length."

"Truly?" Serena asked naïvely. She was pleased to think someone had spoken favourably of her to Jamie, and a pale blush of colour suffused her cheeks. "But it is too absurd. Why, I only chatted with the gentleman for a few moments. How extraordinary that anyone would remark it."

"Not at all. You must remember you are in London now, Serena, and must behave most cautiously. Gossip is a favourite pastime here, and everything and anything is grist for the rumour mill, especially when it concerns a notorious fellow like Rotterdam. I hope you will have a care, for it cannot do you good to have your name linked with his."

"I apprehend the purpose of your visit is to deliver something in the nature of a reprimand, Lord Lynton," Lady Trevelyan said stiffly.

Jamie stirred uncomfortably. "No, of course not. I would never be so presumptuous. It is only that when I heard Serena's name so casually mentioned with Rotterdam's, and in White's of all places . . . well, I merely thought I should drop a word of warning in your ear. I feared you might not realize—"

"Is that the reason you called, Jamie?" Serena interrupted, unable to hide the disappointment in her brown eyes.

"Well, no, not entirely. Of course I wished to see you," he muttered in some confusion, suddenly longing to be miles away. He tried to make amends. "After all, we are neighbours. We country people must have a care for one another. Do you not agree, Lady Trevelyan?"

Marjorie laid aside her needlepoint, and the look she directed at James was noticeably cool. "Quite, my lord, but although I appreciate your concern, I must believe it to be misplaced. I have yet to hear it said Lord Rotterdam has ever trifled with a respectable young lady, and I think there can be no doubt that my daughter is eminently respectable."

"None at all! Good heavens, surely you cannot believe I meant to imply otherwise?" he asked, flushing at the rebuke. "You must know how fondly I regard Serena. Indeed, did I not regard her almost as a sister, I should not have ventured to say a word."

"It is most kind of you to concern yourself, my lord, but as I said, I believe it is hardly necessary."

"I think you cannot understand, Lady Trevelyan. If you but knew the earl's reputation—"

"I do not feel this is a subject that should be discussed before Serena," Marjorie interrupted. She turned to her daughter and, in a tone that brooked no argument, ordered her to leave them.

"But Mama—" Serena began.

"I shall speak with you directly," Lady Trevelyan said, rising from her chair. She waited patiently until Serena had left the room and then turned to James, frost in her eyes. "Reputations are such fragile things, are they not? Perhaps it is your own for which you should have a care. As you say, my lord, we are neighbours and must look after one another, so I know you would not take it amiss were I to hint that lately there have been rumours regarding your own conduct with a certain lady of, shall we say, somewhat doubtful virtue?"

James, who had risen courteously to his feet, now flushed angrily. He had known it would not be easy to conduct this interview, but he had never dreamed Lady Trevelyan would so resent his concern that she would cast aspersions on his own behaviour. To his mind, there could be no comparison between Mrs. Tallant and Rotterdam. The widow might not be received in the first circles, but she was certainly a great deal more respectable than a rake like the earl! He bowed stiffly. "I fear I have overstayed my welcome and must take my leave. No, please do not trouble yourself. I shall find my own way out."

"As you will," Lady Trevelyan agreed, and remained standing by her chair.

James hesitated, experiencing a sudden and compelling urge to protect Serena. None of this was her fault. She might look the epitome of a sophisticated young lady in her pretty yellow gown and with her hair pinned up so neatly, but he wasn't fooled. She was still the sweet and innocent little girl who had tagged after him, generously offering her heart with both hands. She would always be dear to him, and he could not in good conscience leave her to the likes of Rotterdam.

He smiled ruefully, searching for the right words to convince Lady Trevelyan. "I know I have inadvertently offended you, my lady, and I offer you my humble apologies, but I most earnestly beg you not to allow your annoyance with me to blind you to the truth. Rotterdam's attentions, if not checked, could do Serena irreparable harm."

Marjorie was not unmoved by Lynton's obvious sincerity and, while regretting the necessity of setting him at a distance, realized it was imperative that she do so. "I believe you mean well, James, but you must allow me to judge what is best for my daughter. As for Lord Rotterdam, well, perhaps you misunderstand his intentions. He is, despite his reputation, a gentleman—and extremely eligible. Should he offer for Serena, it would be considered an exceptional match."

"*Offer for her?*" James gasped.

"It is not outside the realm of possibility," she replied, smiling at his amazement. "Now, you must excuse me. Pray remember to give my regards to your mother."

James nodded, not trusting himself to speak. He somehow found himself in the hall, where Serena waited. She had busied herself with rearranging the flowers in a vase adorning the mahogany table and was not immediately aware of his presence.

He watched her for a moment. The sun coming in the high windows silhouetted her slender shape, and it was with something of a shock that he suddenly realized Serena had a very lovely figure. He brushed the notion aside. She was still impossibly young, he thought, though he could see how a man like Rotterdam might be tempted. She was so sweetly innocent and had not yet learned the art of dissembling. However, a few months in London would no doubt give her a veneer of sophistication. The thought saddened him, and he very much wished Lady Trevelyan had left Serena at Malmesbury where she belonged.

She turned suddenly, catching sight of him. "Jamie? What is it? You look so strange!"

"Do I?" he asked, shaking his head. "Forgive me, then. I fear I am a trifle preoccupied. Your mother and I have had a small disagreement."

"About Lord Rotterdam?" she asked, watching him closely.

"Yes, minx. I cannot think him a suitable person for you to know, but Lady Trevelyan disagrees."

"Well, I must say, I thought him very amusing," Serena said, glancing up at him with a mischievous smile as she linked her arm through his.

"Amusing! Gad, you are not fit to be let out alone," he muttered without thinking. They were a dozen feet from the door and he was aware of the footman waiting to hand him his hat. He halted their steps and looked down at her. "Serena, promise me you will have a care when Rotterdam is about. You are too young to understand but—well, you must trust that I know what I am saying."

She almost agreed. The ready words of acquiescence were on her tongue and all she wanted was to smooth away the tiny frown between his eyes. But something within her rebelled, a force stronger than herself and irresistible in its intensity. She heard herself replying lightly, "I see no harm in him. Indeed, my friend Miss Appleby said his attention can only add to one's consequence. Come, Jamie, if you will only cease scowling at me, I shall make you a promise. I shall be on guard against Lord Rotterdam if you promise not to give the gossips cause to talk of you and Mrs. Tallant."

"Mrs. Tallant!" he repeated incredulously. "Serena, you know nothing of the lady. Whatever has got into you to make such an outrageous suggestion?"

"I am not deaf, Jamie, and I left the door ajar. Mama's words carried clearly to the hall, so I heard what she said to you, and I also heard my aunt mention the lady's name last night."

"Whatever you may have heard, let me tell you Mrs. Tallant is a very respectable widow who is struggling to survive on the pittance her husband left her and to cope with her grief at his passing. I am shocked at your insensitivity, Serena. Instead of listening to idle gossip about the lady and condemning her out of hand, you would do a good deal better to spare her a bit of compassion."

Serena swallowed hard. She knew an urge to beg Jamie's pardon, but again a stronger power prevailed and made her lift her chin to ask with disconcerting directness, "Is she grieving, Jamie? I thought she looked rather gay when we chanced to meet in the park."

James, aware of the waiting footman, kept his voice pitched low, but there was no mistaking his anger. It was anger all the more intense because he knew there was some little truth to her words, and criticism from one who had always adored him cut deeply. "You are very young, Serena. No doubt it is beyond your comprehension that a lady might not choose to parade her private emotions in public. When you are a little older you will learn one cannot always judge by appearances."

"I am not so young as you may think, my lord," she replied, disengaging her arm. "And I might offer you the same advice with regard to Lord Rotterdam." She gave him no opportunity to answer but turned and retraced her steps to the drawing-room.

James called her once, but Serena ignored him and he stood grinding his teeth in frustration. The waiting footman, imperfectly concealing a grin, coughed discreetly and offered Lord Lynton his hat.

"COME OUT of there, Cuthbert," Eleazar said softly, addressing the suit of armour that decorated one corner of the hall.

Cuthbert materialized slowly. "I always wondered how it felt to wear one of these things," he said, gesturing towards the armour. "A bit awkward, but I can see the advantages to it."

"You would do far better to study the advantages of following orders," Eleazar warned. "Be very careful, and make no mistake. 'Tis dangerous ground you are treading, and you have already been warned twice about interfering beyond the boundaries permitted. You *must* allow Serena to make her own decisions."

"She will, she will," the old soldier muttered. "I only urged her to stand up to your James. It will do him good."

"You did more than urge her. The words she spoke were more yours than hers, and if you continue disregarding the rules, not only will you jeopardize your own place in Heaven, but you may very well be removed as Serena's guardian."

"They would not dare," Cuthbert fumed, and then added fearfully, "would they?"

"They would indeed. Besides which, your precipitous behaviour may not have precisely the effect you envision. Do keep in mind that James is a chivalrous young man, and I fear you may have aroused his protective instincts."

"I should hope so. It's time and past he started having a care for Serena. If he had been a military man—"

"Towards Mrs. Tallant," Eleazar interrupted rudely. When he had Cuthbert's full attention, he explained more gently, "The more everyone disparages the widow, the more James will feel compelled to offer the lady his protection. Many subsequent scenes like this and we shall have the lad offering for her before we know it."

CHAPTER SIX

SERENA DID NOT SEE Jamie for a fortnight, and his absence weighed heavily on her heart. Not even her court presentation, with all its attendant excitement, had the power to distract her for long. She sailed through that arduous afternoon with a noticeable lack of nervousness, causing her aunt to comment on Serena's remarkable poise. Louisa would have swooned had she known her niece privately considered all the pomp and pageantry of being presented to verge on the ridiculous. Serena viewed the wide-hooped gowns, plumed headdresses and nearly vulgar display of jewellery with considerable amusement. And, after all, any assemblage at which Jamie was not present could not have much importance in her eyes. However, she sensibly kept her thoughts to herself and behaved with such exquisite charm she brought tears to her mother's eyes and made her aunt extremely proud.

Once the presentation was past, Serena was able to enter into all the delights of London Society. She was seldom at home, attending any number of routs, balls and musicales in the company of her mama and aunt. In the afternoons, she dutifully paid morning calls, but at five o'clock she was generally allowed to drive in the park with her friend Miss Appleby. Serena went eagerly, hoping to catch a glimpse of Jamie, were it only to see him with Mrs. Tallant, but even that small consolation was denied her, and she soon found herself bitterly regretting having taunted him. She joined Cressida as usual on Thursday, however, and though the top was down on the carriage, and the weather unexpectedly pleasant, she was still downcast and so confided in her friend.

"It is too vexing," Cressida agreed absently, her eyes busily scanning the passing carriages. "I have not seen Rotterdam, either. I suppose the problem is that we are not allowed to frequent the sort of places where we might reasonably expect to encounter them."

"What sort of places?" Serena asked curiously.

"Oh, gambling hells and such," Cressy replied airily. "Have you heard of Lady Montebanks? She has a house in Curzon Street and sends out invitations to what she chooses to call select card parties, but they are really open to anyone with a fat purse and a penchant for faro. I have heard Rotterdam is frequently there." She turned and grinned at Serena. "It is also said the gentlemen are entertained by a number of attractive young ladies of questionable morals."

Serena blushed slightly. For all she was becoming accustomed to Cressy's frank way of speaking, she was still shocked on occasion and she knew her friend found it amusing. Trying to mimic Cressy's sophistication, she murmured, "Well, the earl may frequent such haunts, but I am almost certain Jamie would not. He does not care much for gambling."

"Perhaps not, my dear, but Mrs. Tallant does, and I have it on excellent authority that last evening your Jamie was the widow's escort, and very attentive he was," she said, watching Serena closely. She was fond of the girl, but there were times when her friend's belief in Lord Lynton's perfection irritated her beyond reason. To hear Serena tell it, the gentleman was very nearly a saint.

Cressida saw the crushed look in Serena's eyes before she turned her head, and was instantly contrite. She laid a consoling hand on her arm. "Of course, it means nothing. Gentlemen must have their little amusements, you know. And only consider, my dear. If Lord Lynton truly cared about the lady, he would most certainly not agree to her presence in such a disreputable house."

Serena believed there was some truth in Cressy's words and took what comfort she could from them. She waved at a passing carriage and turned back to her friend. "Well, it does not help either of us. Neither your mama nor mine would agree to our visiting a—a gambling hell, even if we were acquainted with Lady Montebanks." She saw the speculative gleam in Cressy's eyes and added hurriedly, "Do not even think it! Why, to be seen in such an establishment would sink us beyond redemption."

Cressida, who had been entertaining just such a notion, looked downhearted, but reluctantly agreed. "You are correct, of course. Someone would be bound to tell Mama. If only there were some manner in which we could disguise ourselves...."

"I will not consider it," Serena said firmly, and in an effort to distract her friend pointed out an exquisitely clad older man. "Look, there is Mr. Eldridge waving at us."

The gentleman she indicated had been standing a little off the lane, animatedly conversing with a military officer, but he glanced up as their carriage passed, doffed his hat, and gestured for them to come about.

"Harry Eldridge?" Cressy questioned, looking at her friend with new respect. "I say, Serena, you are flying high if you've attracted the attention of someone like Eldridge. No title, of course, but he is extremely wealthy and I cannot tell you how many ladies would swoon were he to glance in their direction! Where did you meet him?'' She leaned forward and directed her groom to turn the carriage.

Serena laughed. ''At Lady Lecompte's—you were at Mrs. Newcombe's musicale that evening. But you cannot be serious, Cressy. Why, he is nearly old enough to be my papa, and though he danced with me once, I suspect he was merely being kind.''

''If you believe that, you have a great deal to learn about men, my dear. Harry Eldridge has been described as many things, but kind is not one of them—and he is an intimate of Rotterdam's.''

''Well, it does not signify. The only gentleman who matters to me is Jamie.''

''Jamie, Jamie, Jamie! Good heavens, do you never think of anything else? No, do not answer,'' Cressy warned at Serena's unrepentant smile. ''But have a care for me. I should like to renew my acquaintance with Mr. Eldridge. I met him last year several times, but this is the first I've seen of him this Season. He must have just returned to Town.''

Their carriage drew to a halt beside the waiting gentlemen, and Mr. Eldridge, drawing his friend forward, smiled at them both. He was a little acquainted with Miss Appleby. In truth, he thought her a fetching filly, but too warm-blooded for his taste. And it was well known amongst the ton that she had her sights set on Rotterdam. That was as foolish as a dog baying at the moon, he thought, but it was hardly his place to counsel the chit. Had she been alone, he would not have bothered to acknowledge her, but she was with Miss

Trevelyan, and that young lady held an irresistible attraction for him. She was a plum ripe for the picking.

"Good afternoon, Mr. Eldridge," Cressida said, extending her hand for his salute. She delicately wet her lips with her tongue and widened her eyes, a pose she had practiced in the looking-glass and was convinced was the height of seductiveness.

"Miss Appleby," Harry said, bending over the delicate hand and wondering what the devil the girl was up to. But the effect was not lost on Captain Stewart, who instantly demanded an introduction. Harry presented him to both young ladies, all the while wishing he could contrive some means of getting Miss Trevelyan alone. She, however, was sitting primly, listening intently to her friend's artless chatter—though her large eyes seemed to sparkle with amusement.

"Tell me, Mr. Eldridge," Cressy said, tapping him lightly on the shoulder with the tip of her parasol, "shall you go to Mrs. Hertford's masquerade ball a week next Thursday?"

"Possibly," he drawled, reluctantly turning his eyes from Miss Trevelyan. "I have an invitation, of course, but am undecided. Do you plan to attend, Miss Appleby?"

"La, sir, I have not received a card, though I hear it promises to be excessively diverting...." she said, sighing regretfully.

Captain Stewart smiled flirtatiously up at her. "I am invited, Miss Appleby, and would consider it an honour to provide you escort if you would but consider it," he offered eagerly.

Cressy laughed and turned to Serena. "Is it not tempting, my dear? Do we dare?"

"I do not think—" Serena began, but Eldridge interrupted her.

"We could form a small party, Miss Trevelyan, and I am certain you would find it *très* amusing. Have you ever been to a masquerade? Imagine everyone masked and free to speak and behave as they will! I can promise you an evening you will not soon forget."

Serena was truly shocked. It was an outrageous proposal and quite improper, but Mr. Eldridge had suggested it as casually as though he were inviting them for a drive in the park. Had he been less assured, or perhaps a few years younger, Serena would not have hesitated to give him a crushing set-down. Only the small doubt that she might be overly prudish and provincial in her notions tempered her reply. "I believe you must be jesting, sir, and know we could not consider attending such an affair. And in any event, we are promised to Lady Palmerston."

"Why, nothing could be more fortuitous. She is Mrs. Hertford's neighbour, and her balls are always such a sad crush, not to mention intolerably boring. I dare say you would not be missed if you slipped away for an hour or two. What do you say, Miss Trevelyan?"

Serena stared at him. "I say you are incorrigible, sir, and I could not possibly agree to such a scheme—"

"Do not let us be hasty, Serena," Cressy interrupted, and turned a glowing smile on Eldridge. "Forgive my friend, Mr. Eldridge. It is her first Season and she has not yet learned the ways of the more stylish members of the ton. Might we let you know? I could send a note round to your lodgings."

"A billet to the Belle Sauvage Inn, Ludgate, will find me," Eldridge replied with a mocking smile.

"I shall send word, then, if we are able to meet you," Cressy said, demurely lowering her eyes.

"At least you leave us with some small vestige of hope," Captain Stewart said, stepping back from the carriage. "I shall appeal to the saints to decide you in our favour."

"I suspect the saints are not much in your line, Captain," Cressy retorted with a laugh. Motioning the groom to drive off, she waved a gloved hand. "Until the next time, gentlemen."

"Have you run mad, Cressida Appleby?" Serena whispered furiously as the carriage pulled away. "Whatever possessed you to—"

"Oh, Serena, do not be such a prig!" Cressy interrupted with a giggle. "This is the answer to our prayers. You did say you wished to see Jamie, did you not?"

"Yes, but what has that to do with Mrs. Hertford's masquerade? I have heard Aunt Louisa speak of the lady and she is not considered at all respectable. Honestly, Cressy, I was never more embarrassed in my life and I dread to think what Mr. Eldridge and the captain must be saying of us."

"Why, only that we are very dashing young ladies and not above a little excitement. And your Jamie, my dear Serena, will be at the masquerade. Now what have you to say?"

"I do not believe you! Why, I have heard Lady Lynton say a dozen times she does not approve of masquerades. James would not—"

"Serena, need I remind you Lady Lynton is not in Town? I suspect your Jamie is doing any number of things his mama would not approve of, and if the widow wishes to attend, well, I am very sure she is capable of persuading him to escort her. Think of it, my dear. She will be there, dancing and flirting with James. Are you going to sit tamely by and do nothing?''

"Very likely," Serena replied drily. "I fail to see what else I can do. Even if I were to agree to such a mad proposal, what good would it serve? Jamie would be furious with me—"

"Which would make him forget the widow, at least for one evening!" Cressy interrupted. "And better for him to be angry with you than not to think of you at all. Oh, Serena—don't you see? The possibilities are endless. Who knows what might happen?"

SERENA, despite Cressida's most persuasive arguments, remained firm in her refusal to have aught to do with such a mad scheme. Nothing might have come of it had not Lady Marcham fallen ill.

Louisa had been feeling poorly on Wednesday morning, and by the time Serena returned from her drive with Cressida, she had retired to her rooms. She complained of a headache and felt feverish, but insisted she was only a little tired and there was nothing to be concerned about. But when she failed to join the family for dinner, and sent word down that they should attend the theatre without her, Lady Trevelyan hurried up to her sister's rooms.

She found Louisa sitting up in bed, her eyes and nose an unbecoming red, her voice sounding rather strained. Marjorie sat beside her and laid a hand across her sister's brow. It felt unnaturally warm to her touch and she suspected a fever.

"How long have you been feeling out of sorts, Louisa?"

"Just a few days. It's nothing, Marjorie, and I do wish you and Serena would go on to the theatre. I shall be better tomorrow—'' She broke off as a fit of coughing shook her slender shoulders and then lay back against the pillows, her eyes watering.

"This is more than just tiredness, Louisa. Does your throat pain you?"

"A little," she murmured, a delicate hand rubbing at her neck just below the ear. "But it's only a summer cold and I would not have it spoil your visit...."

"I shall soon think you delirious if you continue talking such nonsense. Spoil our visit, indeed! How could you think I would leave you in such a state? I have already sent word to the Muncasters that we shall not join them this evening, and as soon as I leave you, I am sending for your doctor. Does Pritchard have his direction? Good. Now, do not argue with me," she added as her sister tried to protest. She rose, straightened the coverlet about Louisa and smiled tenderly. "You were never able to best me in an argument, you know, so do not exhaust yourself with trying. There will be time enough to consider our plans when we hear what the doctor has to say."

Marjorie hurried downstairs, ordered Pritchard to dispatch a footman for the doctor, and joined her daughter in the sitting-room.

"How is she, Mama?" Serena asked, looking up from her embroidery.

"Worse than she imagines, I fear. If I am not much mistaken, your aunt is coming down with the measles."

"Measles? Good heavens, but how—?"

"Lydia Selby," Marjorie interrupted with a sigh. "I persuaded poor Louisa to visit her with me, for it has been years since we met, and of course dear Lydia paraded her children for my inspection. Six, if you can

credit it, and all girls! Lydia did tell us the youngest had
just recovered from measles, and now I suspect one of
the others must have been sickening and passed it on to
your aunt. Was there ever anything so vexing?''

"Oh, poor Aunt Louisa! Is there anything I can do?''

"Nothing, until the doctor arrives." Marjorie sighed
and pulled the bell rope. She ordered tea for herself and
Serena, then directed the maid who served it to take
another pot with honey up to her sister. "And, Mary,
tell Mrs. Moppit I should like a word with her."

The housekeeper appeared a few minutes later. "You
wished to see me, my lady?'' she asked. The words were
polite, and she bobbed a curtsy of sorts, but her manner was surly.

Marjorie chose to overlook it and spoke as pleas-
antly as she could. "I believe my sister is coming down
with the measles, although we cannot be certain until
the doctor has seen her, but if I am correct she will need
continuous nursing. I shall undertake to do most of it,
but I shall require some assistance."

"I knew there was trouble brewing. Like as not we
shall have all the girls coming down sick—"

"I am certain there must be someone among the staff
who has already had the disease. Please be so good as
to find out. That is all, Mrs. Moppit."

The housekeeper bit her lip, mumbled agreement,
and retired. Marjorie shook her head. "That woman is
impossible and I cannot think how Louisa abides her."

"Annie says she is most disagreeable," Serena
agreed, pouring a cup of tea for her mother. "Mama, I
had the measles. Perhaps I could help you, if you would
tell me what must be done."

"Thank you, darling, but I do not think it will be necessary, and I am quite certain your aunt would not wish it."

A tap on the door heralded the arrival of Doctor Phineas Pilman. He was a small man, of indeterminate age and slight bearing. He peered at Marjorie over a pair of spectacles perched on the bridge of his beakish nose, his gaze never wavering as he listened to a catalogue of Lady Marcham's complaints.

Doctor Pilman, in a surprisingly deep and melodious voice, agreed it sounded much like the onset of measles, and Marjorie led him up to her sister's rooms.

Serena, left alone, said a brief, silent prayer for her aunt's speedy recovery, and then occupied herself with her embroidery. But it wasn't very long before the door opened again and her uncle strode into the room. He was startled to see Serena seated near the fireplace, her dark head bent over her needlework.

"Why, what is this? I am certain Louisa told me you were all engaged to attend the theatre this evening."

"We were, but Aunt Louisa is not feeling well and Mama fears it is the measles. She sent for Doctor Pilman and they are abovestairs with my aunt now."

"Measles! Egad, but how is that possible? Louisa is never ill and she seemed quite as usual when I left her this morning—" He broke off, hearing voices in the hall, and turned to see his sister-in-law entering with the doctor.

"Sylvester, I am glad you are returned," Marjorie said with a warm smile, and quickly crossed the room to give him her hand. "I am afraid we have some sad news."

"Serena was just telling me," he replied, giving the doctor a brief nod. "Is it measles, then?" He kept hold of Marjorie's hand and his eyes implored her to say otherwise.

"It is, but do sit down and allow Doctor Pilman to explain it. I believe a cup of tea will do us all good." She seated herself and indicated for the gentlemen to do likewise. Marjorie dispensed the tea and listened quietly as the doctor spoke reassuringly to her brother-in-law. She disliked Sylvester's pale colour, but he seemed to regain some of his usual insouciance when Pilman stressed that he had handled several cases of adult measles and that under his expert care, Lady Marcham should recover her good health within a fortnight.

"I have bled her, so all that is required is some careful nursing—and Lady Trevelyan will see to that. I see no cause for alarm," the doctor added a bit pompously, before draining his cup and setting it carefully on the mahogany table. "Now I must beg to be excused. I do not anticipate any problems, but I shall call in again tomorrow to see how Lady Marcham is progressing."

"Much obliged to you, Doctor," Sylvester said, rising and extending his hand, his hearty bluffness masking a very real concern. "Marjorie, will you show the doctor out while I just run up and have a word with Louisa?"

Lady Trevelyan agreed and added her expressions of gratitude before escorting the doctor to the door. Serena remained where she was, sensing her uncle would wish to be private with his wife. She helped herself to another cup of tea, wondering if there was anything she could do to be of help.

Marjorie returned and took the seat opposite, stretching out a hand to her daughter. "Well, I know you must be disappointed at missing the theatre this evening—"

"Oh, Mama! That hardly matters when Aunt Louisa is ill!"

"Your attitude is commendable, my dear, but neither your aunt nor I wish you to be restricted to the house while she is recovering. There is little you could do, and we both feel you should attend as many engagements as possible. Now, tomorrow morning we must send round a note to Mrs. Appleby. It occurred to us that you and Cressida receive invitations to many of the same parties and I am nearly certain Mrs. Appleby would not object to chaperoning you both." She sighed and rubbed a tired hand across her brow. "Of course, she is not the ideal person to have charge of two lovely young ladies, but I know I can trust you to behave with all propriety."

"YOU CANNOT MEAN to cry off now," Cressy wailed on Thursday of the following week, having got Serena alone in an alcove at Lady Palmerston's. "I sent a note round to Mr. Eldridge promising to meet him at ten!"

"Well, you should not have done so. I told you I would have nothing to do with this madness."

"But that was before your aunt took ill. I was certain you would have no objection now. You said your mama and Lady Marcham would keep too close an eye on you to permit your slipping away, but now—oh, Serena, don't you see? This is like a gift from the gods. Mama is in the card room and she will not look for us again before midnight. We have two hours and I have everything all arranged."

"But someone would be certain to comment on our absence—"

"Nonsense! Did you not get a good look at the ballroom? Why, there is such a crush one can hardly move, much less notice the absence of two young ladies. Even if someone did, we have only to say we stepped into the gardens for a breath of air, which would not be thought remarkable. Not as long as we are together," she wheedled.

"But if we are caught—"

"We will not be," Cressy assured her. "Now, do come, Serena. Why, this may be your only chance to see Jamie for weeks! Surely you do not truly mean to miss such an opportunity?"

The thought of seeing Jamie was nearly irresistible, and Serena felt a strong urge to give in to the impulse. While she had attended, in the company of Cressy and Mrs. Appleby, several evening engagements, she had remained at home during the day with the notion of being useful. Consequently, she'd endured several long, boring afternoons. Lady Trevelyan refused absolutely to allow her near the sickroom, and as her mama spent nearly all her time there, Serena was left to her own devices. Time had hung heavily on her hands, and she'd found herself missing Jamie acutely.

She'd remembered all too clearly the summer she'd been thrown from her horse and badly turned her ankle. She had been the invalid then, laid up for nearly a fortnight and spending her days in the sunny front parlour with her foot propped up on a stool. Her recuperation would have been intolerable except for Jamie. It had been her own fault, he'd said, for rushing her fences. But he had ridden over every day, bringing her flowers and books, and playing endless games of chess with her. She smiled, recalling the number of times she'd beaten him, suspecting he had deliberately let her win. Dear Jamie. He had made every day such a delight, she'd been almost regretful when her ankle had grown strong enough to bear her weight.

"Serena!" Cressy hissed, recalling her attention. "I am leaving. Are you coming or not?"

"You would not go alone!"

Cressy smiled, with a taunting, deliberate look that said she most certainly would. "I am going to find Rotterdam. You may choose to stay here, if you will." She spun on her heel and hurried down the long corridor. She had visited Lady Palmerston before and, thanks to an amusing flirtation with a young lieutenant, knew her way down the back stairs and out into the garden.

Serena hurried after her, telling herself she could not allow Cressy to go alone, but propelled by a strong urge to see Jamie. She caught up with her friend on the steps, and obedient to Cressy's whispered warning, crept silently after her. They eased the door open, careful to leave it slightly ajar, and slipped into the garden. The air felt deliciously cool after the overheated ballroom, and the heady scent of the flowers filled the night. Serena felt a shiver of excitement and willingly followed Cressida round the house and through the gate.

"I told Mr. Eldridge we would meet him here," Cressy whispered, pausing near the front of the house. Carriages were still arriving in the street for Lady Palmerston's ball and she was careful to keep within the shadows.

Serena found herself hoping Mr. Eldridge would keep the tryst. After she'd come this far, the thought of turning back without seeing Jamie was unbearable. She was half-convinced the gentleman would not appear, when a dark figure suddenly loomed up beside them.

"Ladies, I bid you good evening," he whispered.

"Did you bring the dominoes and masks as I asked?" Cressy demanded.

"But of course, my dear," he replied, handing each girl a dark, hooded domino and mask. "No one will recognize you in these."

Serena knew it was wrong, but she couldn't repress the surge of anticipation that shot through her. She quickly slipped on the domino, tying it securely, and then the mask. They effectively hid her hair and most of her face, and feeling a trifle more secure, she accepted the arm Mr. Eldridge offered.

"Ready, ladies?" With a young girl on either arm, he led them towards the street and strolled nonchalantly past the waiting carriages. Serena faltered, but he drew her along, and after a moment she realized no one was paying them any attention. They passed on to Mrs. Hertford's house, where dozens of candles illuminated the windows and loud music and laughter could be heard even in the street. A noisy party alighted from a carriage just before them, and they followed the revellers up the steps and into the spacious hall. Mr. Eldridge presented his card of invitation to the waiting footman, and they were waved up the wide stairs.

There was no grand receiving line here, and Serena hesitated again at the top of the steps. The huge ballroom lay before them, nearly as crowded as Lady Palmerston's but more dimly lit. Dozens and dozens of couples were dancing, indecently close, it seemed to Serena, and all of them masked. Then a young girl in a scandalously transparent gown, clinging to an elderly gentleman, passed close to them. She knocked clumsily into Serena, who smelled the fumes of whisky on the girl's breath and drew back.

"Do not stare, my dear. It is considered most impolite at a masquerade," Eldridge whispered, a trace of amusement in his voice.

"Is that you, Eldridge?" a tall gentleman in a dark blue domino enquired, pausing before them. "I had all but given you up."

Serena recognized Captain Stewart's voice and smiled nervously, but his attention was all for Cressida and he swept her off to join the couples on the crowded floor.

"Shall we?" Eldridge asked, bowing before her and extending his hand.

Serena went reluctantly into his arms. This was vastly different from waltzing in the brightly lit rooms of Almack's before the scrutinizing stares of the dowagers. Eldridge was holding her far too closely. She could feel his warm breath on her neck and shuddered to think what Mama would say. Uncomfortable and nervous, she moved clumsily, stumbling twice as she tried to search the passing faces for a glimpse of Jamie.

Eldridge drew her away to a secluded alcove and indicated she should be seated on the delicate sofa. "Nervous, little one?" he murmured, bending over her. He placed a gloved hand beneath her chin, tilting it up. "There is no reason to be, I promise you. I think perhaps a glass of champagne will do much to settle you. Will you wait here while I fetch a cup?"

Serena managed to nod and made an effort to smile, hoping he would not notice the way her hands trembled. As soon as he moved away, she rose from her seat and edged along the wall, hoping to find either Jamie or Cressy. She never should have come, she thought, and with a pang remembered her mama saying she trusted her to behave with propriety....

"All alone, my pretty one?"

Serena whirled as a pudgy hand reached out for her, but she was not quick enough and found herself pulled into a tight embrace. She struggled to free herself, but the man's arms were like a rope about her and she hammered in vain at his chest.

"Spirit, that's what I like. Give me a gel with spirit," he muttered, raining wet, sloppy kisses on her face while his hands roved down her back and hips.

"Let me go!" she pleaded, averting her face only to feel him nuzzling her neck. "Please, leave me be!" she cried, pulling at his hair. It had little effect, and, nearly desperate, she bit his ear.

He sprang back then with an oath and raised a hand to cuff her. He was stopped by a tall gentleman who seized his hand in mid-air. "I believe the lady does not wish for your attention, Crawford. Find one that's willing."

Serena did not wait to thank her rescuer. A small crowd had turned to watch the scuffle, and there were titters of amusement as she dodged between two gentlemen and rushed towards the door. She had been mad to come, mad to allow Cressy to talk her into such an adventure. Tears streamed down her face and she could barely see. She was nearly at the doorway when she collided with a gentleman and lady just coming in, and losing her balance, fell against a potted tree placed by the door. Its container shattered and she sprawled among the dirt and leaves and fragments of pottery.

"Good heavens, are you hurt?" the gentleman asked, leaning down to help her to her feet.

Serena, recognizing the voice, shut her eyes, praying she might disappear through the floor.

"She looks as if she's going to be ill," she heard someone say in a bored, unconcerned manner. "Too much champagne, no doubt."

"Leave her be, James. The servants will see to her...."

Serena felt his strong hands pulling her to her feet and she swayed dizzily. She longed to bury her face against his shoulder and beg him to take her from this place, but she knew she must not let Jamie recognize her now. Reluctantly she opened her eyes, and doing her best to disguise her voice, murmured, "I—I shall be fine. Please forgive me, sir."

Lord Lynton, keeping a firm arm about her shoulders, turned to his companion. "I think I should see her into a carriage. Go on with the others, Beryl, and I shall join you directly."

"Really, James, I hardly think it necessary..." the widow began. Then, seeing the implacable look in his eyes, she smiled. "Oh, very well. Ever the knight errant. But do hurry back, my dear."

Serena kept her face averted and allowed him to lead her into the hall and towards the stairs. It was quieter there and she paused, pulling away from his hold. "I can manage now, sir. Please go back to your friends."

"Are you certain?" he asked, hating to press his attention on her but unwilling to leave so tiny a lady without escort.

Serena nodded, silently offering fervent thanks that she would be allowed to escape so easily. She took two steps down the stairs and froze. Cressida's voice seemed to fill the hall.

"Serena! Wait! Are you all right?" she cried, crossing the hall. "I saw you fall, but I was across the room and could not reach you."

James was beside her in an instant. A hand like iron gripped her shoulder, spinning her to face him. With his other hand he pushed the hood of her domino off her hair. "Serena? My God, it is you! What the devil are you doing here?"

She swallowed and looked up at him. "I—I was curious—"

"Oh, for the love of Heaven," he muttered. Aware of the strange looks being cast in their direction, he took her arm and urged her down the steps.

Cressy followed, her brows raised as she assessed him. So this was Serena's Jamie. Well, he might look like an angel, but this was no tame fop to be easily brought to heel.

James did not speak until they were outside. He turned on Serena then, fury blazing in his blue eyes. "How did you get here? Do you have a carriage or shall I drive you home?"

Cressy stepped forward. "I beg your pardon, my lord, but our carriage is at Lady Palmerston's and neither of us may leave just yet. Mama will be expecting—" She broke off at the murderous look turned in her direction.

"You, I apprehend, are Miss Appleby?"

His recognition of her could not in any manner be construed as a compliment and Cressy nodded mutely, biting her lip.

Serena laid a hand on his arm. "Please, do not be angry, Jamie. If I could only have a word with you in private—"

"You shall have plenty of words with me on the morrow, miss. Just tell me this. If you were supposed to be at Lady Palmerston's, how did you manage to get into Mrs. Hertford's?"

"Mr. Eldridge had an invitation and he met us at the gate. Jamie, I am so sorry. I know I never should have come. I never realized—"

"You are just the same as ever, Serena—pitching head first into trouble without a thought to the consequences. And with Eldridge, of all people!" Concern for her filled him with unreasoning anger and he spoke more harshly than he'd intended, but when he looked down into her upturned face, some of his fury abated. Serena had removed her mask, and her pale skin glowed softly in the moonlight. Her large eyes appeared to be swimming in unshed tears. "Never mind. We shall discuss this tomorrow. The thing now is to get back to Lady Palmerston's ball before you are missed."

CUTHBERT, sitting on a tree limb that extended just above the walk, chuckled softly. "What say you now, Eleazar?" he asked, peering down at his mentor, who was standing with some dignity beneath the tree. "I said a bit of jealousy was just what we needed. I dare say your James won't be thinking of the widow this evening! Did you see how angry he was to find his precious Serena in such a house? That shows how much he cares about her."

"Of course he cares about the child—there was never a question of that—but this could have unexpected consequences."

"Balderdash. The best defence is attack. James was ignoring Serena, but now he is forced to pay heed."

Eleazar glanced at the retreating form of his charge. "I confess to feeling a certain empathy for him. You charge ahead without due consideration and with a sublime disregard for the rules. You and Serena."

For a brief second Cuthbert looked crushed, and he floated down to rest beside Eleazar. "What is it that worries you?"

"Just go warily. This is not Malmesbury, where Serena can play her tricks to gain James's attention, and no harm done. This is London, Cuthbert, and you have stirred up a hornets' nest this night."

"But that is just as I intended," the old soldier said with a laugh. "A perfect campaign, perfectly executed."

"A hornets' nest," Eleazar repeated softly. "And there is no telling who might get stung."

CHAPTER SEVEN

SERENA AND CRESSIDA were able to slip into Lady Palmerston's ballroom without attracting undue attention. Only one or two persons questioned their absence, and to those Cressy replied with studied nonchalance that they had merely stepped outside for a breath of air. "Do you not find it unbearably stuffy in here?" she asked Lieutenant Knapp, peering up at him from over the top of her fan.

"Indeed, Miss Appleby, but not sufficiently to keep me from requesting the honour of leading you out."

Serena watched her friend walk off with the lieutenant just as though nothing untoward had occurred. No one had remarked their absence, but Serena still expected their shameless behaviour to be exposed at any moment. She could imagine the incredulous faces and the buzz of gossip that would quickly circulate. Worst of all was the vivid memory of Jamie's shock and anger, which she could not erase from her mind. She managed a dutiful smile for the few young gentlemen she danced with, and made polite conversation with the matrons who enquired kindly for her mother and aunt, all the while wishing she could leave at once.

She watched Cressy dancing with one gentleman after another, for the girl never lacked partners, and wondered that there was nothing in her friend's demeanour to indicate she felt even the slightest remorse.

Cressy laughed, chattered and used her fan to such good effect that she was the centre of an admiring group. Indeed, so popular was her friend that Serena had no opportunity for private conversation until just before they were to go in to dinner.

Cressida, excusing herself from her friends, linked her arm in Serena's and suggested they retire for a few moments. She led the way to a small withdrawing-room on the second floor, and after making certain they were quite alone, hastily shut the door. "Gracious, Serena, can you not strive to appear more cheerful? Anyone watching would suspect you have just suffered the greatest bereavement!"

"And that is precisely how I feel!" Serena snapped, her patience at an end and her head throbbing unbearably.

"Well, I am sure there is no need to advertise it to the world," Cressy replied, studying her friend critically. "Really, my dear, I fear you are repining too much on this. It was distressing, certainly, but when all is said and done, there was no harm—and you did manage to see your Jamie, while I never caught a glimpse of Rotterdam. The captain kept me so close I never had the opportunity to speak to another soul, but I am positive Rotterdam was present, for I heard his name mentioned. Now, do not look at me like that. I did not mean to imply that it was in any way your fault—"

"Cressy," Serena interrupted, suppressing an urge to shake her friend until her pretty ear-bobs rattled. "You are mad. Quite, quite mad. I have suspected it before but now I am entirely convinced." She sighed and wearily sank down into one of the mahogany armchairs. "When I think of what Mama will say... It is likely she will forbid me ever to see you again, and I should not be surprised if she wishes me to return to Malmesbury at once. It is no more than I deserve."

"But you cannot mean to confide in your mother!" Cressy cried, horrified. She rapidly crossed to Serena's side and knelt beside the chair. "My dear, you have not considered. Why, there cannot be the slightest need. We behaved badly, I will own, but even you must admit we have learned our lesson. I know you would never try such a thing again, so what would be the point in confessing? It is done and best forgotten."

"Even if I were so lost to all propriety as to listen to you, you are forgetting Jamie. He will consider it his duty to tell Mama what has occurred."

"Surely he would not do anything so underhanded? Why, it would cause you the gravest trouble, and however angry he was, he cannot wish to see you in disgrace."

"No, but he would believe he is acting to protect me. He must think I am incapable of exercising good judgement," Serena said, swallowing hard to dislodge the sudden tightness in her throat.

"Serena, you must persuade him otherwise! Why, if he tells Lady Trevelyan what occurred, she will certainly speak to Mama." The thought of what her own mama might say caused Cressy to suddenly grow pale. For all her laxity in chaperoning her daughter, Mrs. Appleby would not take kindly to learning of this evening's escapade. Cressy redoubled her efforts.

"Listen, Serena, you must be on the watch for Jamie tomorrow and not allow him a chance to talk to Lady Trevelyan. Beg him to drive out with you and allow you the opportunity to explain everything. Tell him it was all my doing and promise never to do such a thing again.

He will not wish to persecute you and ruin your first Season. He is not unreasonable, is he?''

"No, of course not—"

"Then you must convince him to be sensible. Serena, if Mama learns of this, she will send me home, and I could not endure it. It does not bear thinking of. Do you want me to come help you persuade Jamie tomorrow? I could tell Mama that—"

"No!" Serena cried sharply, her head coming up. "I am sorry, Cressy, but I should prefer to speak to Jamie alone. I promise I shall do what I can to convince him, but I do not think it would help at all to have you present."

"Very well," Cressy said coolly. She rose to her feet. "Come, we had best return to the ballroom before Mama begins looking for us, though I do not know how I shall contrive to behave normally. Gracious, all this fuss just because I agreed to help you try to see your precious Jamie! Perhaps you should point out to him that this is really all his fault. If he had called on you, as he should have done, you would not have been put to such lengths to see him."

Serena closed her eyes briefly, such logic being beyond her own comprehension. She imagined Jamie's consternation should she present him with such a spurious argument. The corners of her mouth tilted up, and then she giggled.

"Serena?" Cressy said with a tinge of alarm, wondering if her friend was growing hysterical.

"Jamie...Jamie would be so astonished to learn he was at fault," Serena said, and clutched her side weakly as laughter overcame her.

SERENA WAS NOT entirely immune to Cressy's pleas, but she had given no promises. She was still undecided when she returned home, and though she wished to confide in her mother, she realized to do so would have dire consequences for her friend. For once her inner voice was of no help, remaining strangely silent.

Fate seemed to take the decision out of her hands. Pritchard informed her that Muriel, Lady Marcham's personal maid, was laid low with the measles. Apparently she had caught the disease before being banished from her mistress's room. Now Lady Trevelyan was nursing both patients with the help of Mary, the only maid on the staff who had suffered measles as a child. Under no circumstances was Serena to be permitted in the sickroom.

The following morning brought little change, and Serena ate breakfast in solitary splendour. When she enquired, Mrs. Moppit grudgingly informed her that trays had been taken up for the ladies and for the master as well. "He insisted on spending as much time with my lady as possible."

"Well, that is kind of him," Serena replied, refusing to be cowed by the truculent housekeeper.

"*Humph.* Like as not, he will be taken sick as well and it will mean more work for us belowstairs."

"But then, that is what you are paid to do, is it not?" Serena asked sweetly. She had the dubious pleasure of seeing a flush spread over Mrs. Moppit's beefy face before the housekeeper abruptly withdrew.

She felt a tiny twinge of remorse. The remark had been unworthy of her and she knew Papa would not have been pleased. He said it was beneath a lady to loose her temper with those not in a position to retaliate. Nor would Papa be pleased to learn of her behaviour the night before. The thought effectively dampened her appetite, and Serena motioned to the waiting footman to remove her plate.

She withdrew to the small parlour near the front of the house and tried to concentrate on her embroidery stitches, but her eyes kept straying to the window. She knew she did not have to fear Jamie's arrival, for both her mother and Aunt Louisa would be denied to all visitors no matter how urgent the request for an audience. However, she had decided to speak to Jamie herself.

An hour passed slowly with little to relieve the tedium, but when Serena finally heard the knocker and Jamie's deep voice in the hall, she immediately regretted he had arrived so soon. For all she wanted to see him, it was with some reluctance that she stepped into the hall. Both Jamie and Pritchard turned in her direction at once.

Jamie bowed deeply. "Good day, Miss Trevelyan. I wished a word with your mother or Lady Marcham, but the butler tells me neither lady is at home?"

"They are not receiving visitors, Jamie," she said, her voice sounding weak to her ears. She swallowed and added in a more normal tone, "Aunt Louisa is ill and Mama is nursing her."

"I am most sorry to hear that. I trust her illness is not of a serious nature?"

"No..." she replied, a trifle disconcerted by his forbidding mien. "At least the doctor has said we need not be unduly alarmed. She is recovering from measles, you see."

"What is this?" Lord Marcham called out, coming down the steps and into the hall. "Thought I heard voices. Lynton, isn't it? How do you do?"

"Good day, sir. I fear I have come at a most inopportune time. Miss Trevelyan was just telling me of the illness in the house."

Sylvester nodded. "Struck my wife all at once. Never seen her laid so low, but my sister-in-law is doing an excellent job of nursing her and we expect to see Lady Marcham restored to us very soon. Now, Serena, your aunt expressly charged me to see that you do not repine. She suggested I take you for a drive, but it occurs to me that if young Lynton here is willing, he might deputize for me."

Serena blushed, but Jamie nodded gravely. "I should be honoured, sir."

"Good, that's settled, then. Step into the drawing-room with me while my niece fetches her hat and gloves."

Serena listened to their fading voices as she hurried up the stairs. It would not do to leave Jamie alone with her uncle for too long. But her fingers were all thumbs and she had to allow Annie to tie the ribbon of her hat and find the matching blue pelisse and gloves. Doing so seemed to take an eternity, but it was only a quarter-hour later when Serena allowed Jamie to hand her into his waiting curricle.

She sat stiffly, staring at the back of the groom and waiting for Jamie to speak. He gave Paddy, his man, curt orders, but then remained quiet. They left the square behind and turned down Oxford Street, but still Jamie did not say a word. His continued silence unnerved Serena, and she stole a look at him from beneath the brim of her bonnet.

He had eschewed a hat and his dark blond curls were slightly disordered by the breeze, but he still looked very serious and his brows were drawn together in a frown.

Jamie had been angry with her before, on numerous occasions, in fact, but he had never remained so for long and she knew him incapable of harbouring a grudge. He must indeed be furious, she thought with a sinking feeling in the pit of her stomach, and wondered if there was anything she could say to ease the tight lines about his mouth.

James, however, was not angry with Serena. He had been appalled to find her at Mrs. Hertford's and deeply shocked to realize how perilously close she had come to ruining herself. But he knew it was not Serena's fault. She was an innocent and should never have been left to the dubious care of Mrs. Appleby and her daughter. He had fully intended to point out to Lady Trevelyan the folly of her ways, however much she might resent his interference, but now that was clearly not possible. He sighed and glanced down at Serena. She looked so forlorn he had not the heart to scold her.

"Well, minx?" he asked at last, making an effort to keep his voice light. "What mischief are you brewing now?"

Startled, Serena looked up at him, her dark eyes filling with relief and her lips forming a tremulous, tentative smile. "None, Jamie, I promise you. I am so very sorry about...about last night," she finished.

"And so you should be," he said. "But I suppose I know where to lay the blame for that escapade. It is just the sort of rig Miss Appleby would consider great fun. I have little doubt that, left to your own devices, you would never have considered such a prank, and I can only deplore your association with that young lady."

Serena bit her lip. This wasn't the Jamie she had romped and cavorted with, the playmate who had willingly rescued her from many scrapes and contrived to protect her from her parents' censure. It seemed Jamie had grown up. The thought saddened her, and even worse was the unfair charge he had levelled against Cressy. She could not allow him to blame her friend when she knew herself to be equally at fault.

Serena faced him squarely, lifting her tiny chin. "That is not true, Jamie. Cressy may have conceived the idea, but I went with her willingly enough."

"Stop looking at me like that, Serena," he ordered, stricken by the hurt in her eyes. "As though I have somehow betrayed you, when all I am trying to do is protect you. Come now, I promise I do not mean to scold, only, my dear, you must realize what a foolish risk you took. Had you been discovered in a house like Mrs. Hertford's, your reputation would have been ruined. It is hardly a fit place for a lady."

"And yet you escorted Mrs. Tallant to the same house," she murmured, staring straight ahead.

It was a leveller and James shook his head, at a loss for words. "That is very different," he said at last.

"Why?" Serena asked, her wide brown eyes searching his.

"Why? I don't know—it simply is! Mrs. Tallant is a widow and she has seen something of the world. She is not as innocent as you or—"

"But she is a lady, is she not?"

"Well of course she is, Serena. What has got into you even to ask such a thing?"

"I am only trying to understand, Jamie. Please tell me why you consider it permissible for Mrs. Tallant to visit Mrs. Hertford's, but terribly wrong of me?"

He ran a gloved hand through his hair and sighed audibly. "Lord, Serena, must you take me up on every word I say? I think we would do well to leave Mrs. Tallant out of this discussion." He did not wish to own that he had been a trifle disconcerted when Beryl had proposed attending the masquerade. He had not lied when he said he considered the house an unfit place for a lady, but Beryl had made his protests seem somehow gauche and provincial, and she had teased him into escorting her.

It was not an evening he wished to remember. Beryl had questioned him closely when he'd returned from escorting Serena to Lady Palmerston's, and she had been plainly annoyed when he'd brushed aside her enquiries. She had left him to cool his heels and had danced with a number of gentlemen, behaving more flirtatiously than he considered proper.

He suspected her behaviour was a ploy to make him jealous, but she had succeeded only in irritating him. He had been on the verge of suggesting that one of her admirers see her home when the widow had returned to his side full of pretty apologies. The rest of the evening had passed off well enough, but there was a coolness between them that he knew was his own fault.

"It appears Mrs. Tallant does not wish to be left out of our conversation," Serena murmured, recapturing his attention. They had turned into the park, and she nodded at the approaching carriage. "That is the widow waving at you, is it not?"

James looked up. It was indeed Beryl, looking particularly fetching on the seat of an open carriage, her tiny poodle perched beside her. He reluctantly ordered Paddy to pull up.

"Good day, my lord," the lady greeted him happily, smiling at him from beneath the wide brim of her stylish green hat. "Such a surprise encountering you here, but I see you have your little friend from the country

with you. Miss...Trevelyan, I believe? Are you enjoying your visit to London, my dear?''

"Very much, thank you," Serena answered quietly,
regretting the necessity of speaking civilly to this woman
who claimed so much of Jamie's time and attention.

"I thought Miss Trevelyan might enjoy a drive
through the park," she heard Jamie explain. "Her
aunt, Lady Marcham, has unfortunately fallen ill and
cannot take her about."

"How sweet of you, James, but then I would expect
no less," Beryl replied, and turned to Serena with a
small laugh. "He is always so thoughtful, I find. Such
a charming attribute in a gentleman. Why, just last
evening he came gallantly to the rescue of a young girl
at a masquerade party." She paused, studying Serena
with frank curiosity. "But perhaps you are aware of
what occurred?''

"How should I be? Surely you know Jamie is far too
modest to speak of such deeds," Serena said, managing to sound credibly composed while twisting her
gloved hands together in her lap.

"You make too much of it, Beryl. Any gentleman
would have done the same," James interrupted, trying
to turn the conversation aside.

"Ah, but you gave none other an opportunity. You
moved so swiftly to the child's aid, one might almost
suppose you recognized the girl. Or perhaps it was just
the close resemblance she bore to Miss Trevelyan? They
are of the same size, I believe?''

"Jamie!" Serena cried, looking up at him with
adoring eyes. "Did you truly help some girl because she
resembled me? That is the nicest thing I have ever
heard! I can hardly wait to tell Mama.''

"Now see what you have done," James said, grinning at Beryl. "I shall have no peace until I tell her every detail!"

"Not a moment's," Serena vowed with an impish grin. "But I shall mind my manners and refrain from plaguing you in the presence of your friend."

Beryl was undecided. She was nearly certain Miss Trevelyan was the same young girl she'd seen at Mrs. Hertford's, yet the thought was scarcely credible. She knew how heavily chaperoned a young lady was during her first Season, and it would have been nearly impossible for Miss Trevelyan to slip away to attend a masquerade.

The poodle beside her yelped at a passing carriage and Beryl reached down a hand to quiet it. "Well, my dears, this absurd dog of mine grows restive and I suppose I must be off. You will not forget we are promised to the Brenermans this evening, James? I am so looking forward to viewing the gardens with you. Miss Trevelyan, a pleasure to see you again."

"I could hardly forget so delightful an engagement," James answered warmly, and received an intimate smile for his pains.

"Mrs. Tallant." Serena nodded and smiled sweetly until the widow's carriage was past, and then she made an unbecoming face. James did not notice and appeared lost in thought. They drove on in silence for some moments until Serena could bear it no longer.

"Jamie?"

"What, minx?" he asked, looking down at her with a bemused smile.

"Thank you for not telling Mrs. Tallant. I could not endure it were she to know the truth."

"It would have served no purpose," he replied abruptly, and turned away from her inquisitive eyes. He would not own it, but he'd felt he could not trust Beryl to keep Serena's secret and had deliberately refrained from confiding in the widow the evening before. That had not been an easy task, for she'd been relentless in her questioning.

Serena laid a gentle hand on his sleeve. "I have placed you in a most awkward situation when all I wished to do was see you. Cressy said she felt sure you would be at the masquerade. I am truly sorry, Jamie."

"Then there is no more to be said, save next time you wish for my company, I suggest you send a note round to my rooms."

She considered his suggestion seriously and then shook her head. "I do not believe Mama would approve," she said. "She would think it too forward of me."

James threw back his head and laughed aloud. "That is rich, Serena! You doubt Lady Trevelyan would approve of your sending me a note, and yet you somehow convinced yourself it was quite proper to attend a masquerade at Mrs. Hertford's. Your logic escapes me."

She grinned, revealing her dimples, and slipped her hand confidently into his. This was her own dear Jamie. "Papa says that ladies' reasoning processes are vastly different from gentlemen's and that it has always been beyond him to understand how Mama's mind works."

"Your papa is a very wise man, and no doubt he would advise me that the easiest solution is for me to call on you more frequently."

"I should like that," Serena said simply, though her heart was racing wildly.

"Good. Now tell me, minx, what are your plans for the next week? Do you go to Almack's?"

"Mama had said I might attend with Mrs. Appleby and Cressy, but if you dislike the notion, Jamie—"

"No, it will do. Just be warned that I shall be there to keep an eye on you and will expect the honour of two dances. You *can* dance, can you not?" he asked, teasing her.

"Of course, Jamie, but do you know we have never danced together?" she said, her eyes aglow with anticipation. "I shall be so excited, I will not sleep a bit until Wednesday!"

"Now that is the most idiotish thing I have ever heard," James said, smiling at her childish enthusiasm, but he sat a little taller in the seat and there was no denying the warm feeling in his chest. It was so ridiculously easy to please Serena.

"I'll tell you what," he added in a spirit of magnanimity, "if you would like it, I will engage to call tomorrow and take you to see Astley's Amphitheatre."

"Oh, Jamie! How splendid. That is where they have the wonderful horses, is it not? I have been longing to go."

"Not just horses, little one, but pony races and sword fights and clowns. You will enjoy it excessively."

"I know I shall, Jamie, particularly if *you* escort me."

BERYL TALLANT returned to her small house on Chesterfield Street determined to bring Lord Lynton up to scratch. She had thought her cavalier treatment of him would inflame his jealousy and bring him quickly to the point, but it had not had the desired effect. Particularly not since Miss Trevelyan's arrival in Town. If any-thing, his ardour seemed to have cooled considerably.

It was obvious she had erred in judging Miss Trevel-yan's potential as a rival. James was far too protective of the girl, and Beryl suspected he cared for her more than he was willing to admit. She sat down at her dressing-table and studied her reflection in the look-ing-glass. Her hair was not as lustrous as it might be and her skin had lost some of its dewy freshness, no doubt a result of the late hours she'd been keeping. Beryl rang for her maid.

She had hours before James would call for her and she intended to make the most of them. She issued curt instructions to Mildred while changing from her car-riage dress to a silk wrapper, and then she hurried down to the kitchen.

Her maid had the rose-water simmering and had al-ready separated six eggs. "What now, miss?"

"Pour out three cups of the rose-water and mix it with three cups of rum," Beryl instructed, and taking up a whisk, whipped the egg yolks into a froth. She set those aside, and then bringing the remaining rose-water to a boil, poured in the six egg whites. She allowed the concoction to simmer for a moment before adding a cup of alum, finely powdered, then beat the mixture until it formed a paste.

"What do you do with that, miss?" Mildred asked curiously. She had already learned more than one trick from her mistress and knew it would be to her benefit to pay strict attention.

"It firms the facial skin," Beryl replied, intent on her work. "Not that I need it, but it is as well to take pre-cautions in Town. The air here is dreadful for one's complexion." She frowned, thinking of Miss Trevelyan's unlined face with its pretty colour.

"You is wrinkling your brow, Miss Beryl," Mildred reminded her. "You said that causes wrinkles and I should tell you."

"Thank you, Mildred," the widow replied, making a conscious effort to smooth her brow. *Think pleasant thoughts,* she told herself. *Think of this evening and how you will bedazzle James.* She settled herself into a chair and instructed Mildred to work the egg-yolk mixture through her hair while she applied the egg-white paste to her complexion.

When the process was complete, she leaned her head on the back of the chair and closed her eyes. "That will be all for now, Mildred. You may leave me." When her hair had dried, it would be rinsed with the rum and rosewater, and her face cleansed. Then she could retire to her bedchamber and rest until it was time to dress—rest and think how to recapture James's attention and put little Miss Trevelyan out of his mind once and for all.

ACROSS TOWN, Retired Major Cuthbert Lacy literally floated on a cloud. "You can't keep a good spirit down," he said, and chortled at his own wit. His Serena was blissfully happy; her high spirits bubbled up inside and spilled about her in trills of delicious laughter. He peered over the cloud and watched as James tenderly handed her down from the carriage. "Ah, matters are proceeding splendidly, just as I predicted."

"It is far from over," Eleazar warned, but even he was encouraged to believe that James might be beginning to see matters in their true light. For too long his charge had been blinded by the lovely widow.

"Oh, certainly," Cuthbert agreed. "We must see them properly wed, of course. When do you think he might offer for her? I don't suppose at Astley's—it hardly seems a romantic setting. Perhaps at Almack's during a waltz? That would be my notion."

"A proposal is not inspired by the locale, but rather by the climate of the heart. It could occur anywhere, at any time."

"Let's hope for Astley's, then. The sooner the better. I always held with striking while the iron is hot."

"I fear you are forgetting a small point or two, Major. James is still engaged to escort the widow to Vauxhall this evening."

"A mere skirmish. You look out for our lad there and see he don't do anything foolish," Cuthbert advised, only half attending. His thoughts were still focused on Serena.

"I shall try," Eleazar murmured after a pause, but his tone was not encouraging and Cuthbert turned to stare at him.

"What are you thinking?" he demanded. "There's a strange look in your eyes. Is it James? Has he said or done something to worry you?"

"No, actually, I was thinking of Napoleon. He was as optimistic as you, and much inclined to predict victory before every battle."

"Can't blame the Little General for that—the man is a brilliant strategist."

"Oh yes, indeed he is, but there is always a Waterloo, and I very much fear ours is still ahead of us."

CHAPTER EIGHT

JAMES AROSE late the following morning, very much regretting the enormous amount of champagne he'd consumed the evening before. The slightest sound exacerbated the pain in his temples, and though he could not recall exerting himself physically, his body ached from head to toe. He sat down at the breakfast-table gingerly, refusing to drink a glass of vinegar or a mug of hot wine, both of which Cecil recommended as being certain to cure the ill effects of intoxication.

"I was not in my cups," James said through clenched teeth, wishing he could crawl into bed and pull the covers over his head.

"No, my lord," Cecil agreed with maddening patience. "Perhaps some black coffee, then?"

"Very well, if it will make you cease plaguing me," he replied. Glancing up, he caught sight of his black dress coat lying on the floor, looking much the way he felt. Large greasy stains decorated the back of it and he could see where it had been badly ripped in several places. "What the devil happened to my coat?"

"It was Caesar, my lord," Cecil said calmly, setting the cup of coffee in front of James. "Apparently you saw fit to bring home some ham in your pockets. The cat sniffed it out at once and there was no wresting the coat from him. I did try, my lord," he added, displaying the long, jagged scratches on his hands.

James flushed guiltily, vaguely recalling an impulse
to bring home something for the cat. There had been so
much food ordered at Vauxhall, and most of it wasted.
He dimly recalled telling Beryl that at such steep prices,
it should be put to use. With a vague notion of providing Caesar a treat, he'd stuffed the thinly sliced ham
into his pockets and then forgotten about it, carelessly
tossing his coat over the chair when he'd returned home.
But that was no reason for Cecil to do battle over it.

"Good Heavens, man, you should have just let the
cat have it. The coat is hardly worth such heroics." He
looked up to where Caesar was contentedly sleeping
atop the bookcase. "Obviously the poor thing must
have been starving. Are we feeding him enough?"

Cecil grunted, eyeing the creature's sleek coat and
remembering the slice of beef that had disappeared the
moment his own back was turned. "The beast is insa-
tiable, sir, and though I hesitate to remind you, this is
the third coat he's ruined in a week. At this rate, you'll
not have a single garment fit to wear."

"Well, we must render unto Caesar that which is
Caesar's," James murmured absently. "I shall see
Weston in a day or two," he added, but his attention
was now on the stack of mail beside his cup. A letter
from his mother rested on top of the pile. He took another sip of the fortifying coffee and slit open the en-
velope, scanning the lines.

He'd had several letters from his mother since her return to Wynyard Park, all of which had imperiously
demanded his presence at home. James had replied
punctually, and with conciliating politeness, but remained firm in his intention to remain in Town until the
end of the Season. Now, apparently, Lady Lynton was

changing her tactics. James frowned, and Cecil, hovering with the coffee pot, refilled his cup.

"Nothing amiss, I hope, sir?"

"No...I do not believe so, but this letter does not sound like Mother," he answered, turning the page to be certain of Lady Lynton's signature and then reading it through again.

His mother mentioned how much she missed him and that there were several matters she felt could not be acted upon without his approval. James lifted his brows at that. His mother was rarely at a loss to know what was best for everyone and had never before deferred to his opinion. She did not mention Beryl, but she did enquire if he had called on Lady Trevelyan and requested her warmest regards be given to her "dear neighbour." She also expressed the hope that Serena was enjoying her Season and that James would not be remiss in escorting his childhood playmate to one or two functions. "It is the least you can do," Lady Lynton wrote. "For depend upon it, the dear girl will not know her way about and will be glad of a friendly face."

James sipped his coffee, wondering if his mother had fallen ill. Far from wishing to be on terms with their neighbours, she had previously done all she could to discourage such a connection and had made it abundantly clear she felt the Trevelyans socially beneath them. James, as had his father before him, merely ignored her wishes.

He loved his mother, of course, and accorded her all due deference and respect, but he was not blind to her faults. Lady Lynton placed great value on rank and wealth and never lost an opportunity to point out to even the most casual of acquaintances her distant connection to royalty on her father's side of the family.

James, despite all his mother's efforts, had inherited his father's disdain for such snobbery. Though he could trace his ancestors back to the Normans, he did not consider it an accomplishment for which he could justly take credit. On the occasions his mother had reminded him of his noble birth, he had teasingly told her he'd had nothing to do with it.

"Beggin' pardon, my lord, but it is drawing on noon," Cecil said, interrupting his thoughts. "And you said yesterday as how you intended to take Miss Serena to Astley's this afternoon."

"Oh, Lord, yes," James groaned, wondering how he could have forgotten. Beryl had not been at all pleased when he'd told her his plans, and it had boded ill for the evening. But she had come round, and instead of sulking as he had half expected, she had been very gay all evening, proposing toast after toast. James had not liked her drinking so much champagne, but George and Angela Brenerman had encouraged her, lifting their own glasses in nonsensical salutes to the King and the Prince of Wales, and James had reluctantly joined them.

The champagne had had its effect. He vaguely recalled escorting the ladies to the rotunda, where they might have a better view of the fireworks, and somehow Angela had been the one to stroll along beside him—an arrangement that did not especially please him, particularly when Beryl and George got lost in the crowd. He'd tried searching for them over the heads of the crowd, but it was impossible to identify anyone in the darkness. His suggestion to Angela that they seek out her brother and Beryl had been met with amused derision, and she'd adamantly refused to leave the rotunda until the fireworks were over. James had been worried. There were a number of rogues in the gardens who could not be trusted to keep to the line, and if Beryl had become separated from George as well, she could be in danger. The incident had sobered James slightly, and as soon as possible he'd rushed Angela back to their table, only to find Beryl and George calmly dining on some of the ham and sipping more champagne.

James had felt foolish for his worry and George had taunted him, but Beryl had thanked him sweetly for his concern and apologized prettily, explaining that the noise and confusion of the rotunda had hurt her head. James had suggested leaving then, but Beryl had only laughed and insisted he sit beside her and sip from her own glass of champagne. It was miraculous, she said, the way it cured her headache and made everything seem so wondrous. It did make her eyes sparkle, he'd thought, accepting the glass and sitting down beside her. Her hand had found its way to his beneath the table, and the perfume she wore filled his senses until he was no longer thinking clearly. And more champagne had followed.

James closed his eyes, wishing once more that he'd been more cautious, though it was difficult to refuse the widow anything when she was in such a mood. He'd been hugely flattered by the way Beryl had attended to his every word and by the adoring looks she'd cast in his direction. But however wonderful he'd felt at the end of the evening, it seemed small compensation for the misery he was now feeling.

He rose stiffly, laid the letter from his mother aside, intending to answer it later, and called to Cecil. "Have I a presentable coat to wear?"

"Yes, my lord," his valet replied, coming into the room. "I've laid out the blue, though you did wear it when you last called on Miss Serena."

"Serena won't mind what I wear," James said with a grin. "She'll be too astonished at the wonders of Astley's to pay any mind to me." He picked up his coffee and strolled into his bedchamber, only to find the tiger-striped tom-cat curled into a sleek ball on top of his coat.

"Get off of there, you abominable beast," he said, grabbing the cat by the scruff of his neck. "Is it your intent to ruin every coat I possess?"

Caesar regarded him with large, unblinking eyes, but settled into his arms with a loud contented purr.

"Don't think to get round me that way," James warned, but he obligingly scratched the beast between the ears before carrying him to the door. "Out with you. Go and catch some mice for your keep."

SERENA WAS READY when James arrived, and though he might think she would not care for what *he* wore, he was very much aware of how fetching she looked in a pretty white walking dress trimmed with pink satin ribbons. There was an aura of freshness and innocence about her that lifted his heart, and he greeted her with a warm smile.

"Jamie, is the day not splendid?" she asked with shining eyes. "We could not have chosen a more perfect time for an outing."

"Completely delightful," he agreed, realizing for the first time how brightly the sun was shining.

Lady Trevelyan stepped into the room and extended her hand. "Good afternoon, James. It is kind of you to take Serena out today."

"My pleasure," he responded, bowing over her hand. He noticed the look of strain about Lady Trevelyan's fine eyes and enquired about her sister.

"She is much improved, thank you, and it is hoped she will be allowed to get up tomorrow. Unfortunately, she still needs me with her today and I cannot accompany you. Serena's maid is also needed here, so I hope you will not object to taking Mrs. Appleby and her daughter with you in our place? She most generously offered to act as chaperon this morning, and it seemed an ideal solution."

James glanced at Serena. Her brown eyes held a pleading look, silently beseeching him to agree. It was an appeal he could not resist, and he turned back to her mother with a ready smile. "As you say, it seems an ideal solution. Am I to call for the ladies or will they meet us here?"

"If it would not inconvenience you, Serena will direct you to Mrs. Appleby's house." Marjorie sighed and added, "I would have invited them here, but we are at sixes and sevens just now."

"Of course. I quite understand," James replied, and after a few more moments of polite conversation, escorted Serena out to his carriage. Fortunately, he was driving the landau, and Paddy had folded the top down so the ladies might enjoy the warm day. He quickly told his coachman of the change in plans and then helped Serena to her seat.

She greeted Paddy warmly, causing him to blush furiously, and then settled happily beside Jamie.

"You little minx," he scolded, helping her into the seat. "Why did you not warn me?"

"I was afraid you would not come," Serena answered with a wide grin. "Besides, Jamie, I am certain that once you come to know Cressy, you will like her immensely. She is—what on Earth?" she cried as a furry animal moved beneath her feet. "Why, Jamie, there is a cat in your carriage."

"Do not touch him," James warned, but Serena was already bending forward and gently lifting Caesar onto her lap.

"He's beautiful, Jamie. Is he yours?" she asked, gently stroking the cat beneath his chin.

"In a manner of speaking," he replied, marvelling at the cat's docile air. "He seems to have adopted me. I put him out this morning and he must have climbed into the carriage when it was brought round. I should tell you he scratched poor Cecil quite dreadfully."

"Cecil? Oh, is he in Town with you? How is he, Jamie? Does he still have that dreadful cough?"

"Fancy your recollecting that," James said, keeping a wary eye on Caesar, but the cat had curled into a ball on Serena's lap and was purring loudly as she ran her gloved fingers behind his ears. "No, he has quite recovered, but he will be pleased to know you remembered him."

"Why, of course I do! How ever could I forget anyone who was as kind to us as Cecil? Do you recall the time we were playing by the river and let the horses wander off? He came and fetched us in the pony cart and never told a soul how careless we were. And that dreadful day when your mama ordered a litter of kittens drowned, it was Cecil who helped me to rescue the dear little creatures."

"Yes, and I remember how you made me trudge the length of Malmesbury trying to find homes for them. Lord, such a fuss you kicked up."

"You did not want them drowned either," she retorted. "And just think, Jamie. Maybe one of them grew into a fine fellow like this one. What do you call him?"

"Caesar, for his delusions of grandeur," he answered with a grin.

"How perfect," Serena crooned, and the cat lifted his head as though he understood her. "Yes, you are a handsome fellow." She glanced up at Jamie. "You must promise to let me know how he does."

"I shall, but for now you must put him down. I believe we have arrived, and if I am not mistaken, there is Miss Appleby waving at you from the window."

"Good Heavens, yes," Serena said, and while James climbed down and walked round the carriage to assist her, she managed to resettle Caesar on the cushioned seat. She gave the cat a last caress, accepted Jamie's waiting hand, and feeling in perfect charity with him, strolled up the walk to greet Cressy.

James was formally introduced to Mrs. Appleby and her daughter, and though he'd expected Cressida to be a shade embarrassed at meeting him again, she was not in the least. She said everything that was proper, but her eyes sparkled with laughter and she treated James much as though they shared a delicious secret. She made a fuss over the cat, suggesting with an impish look that they bring the sweet creature into Astley's with them.

Impertinent girl, James thought, rejecting the idea out of hand, and assuring both young ladies that Paddy would take Caesar home. But he was more than a little amused, and by the time their party reached Astley's, he was in a fair way to understanding why Serena was fond of her friend's company.

Mrs. Appleby was much as he expected, and he could see it was from her that Cressida inherited her fair good looks. The older lady had retained her figure, and though her blond hair was now streaked with grey, James surmised that she had once been a beauty. She was as congenial as she was attractive, but easily diverted and inclined to allow the girls to do much as they pleased. As they were entering the amphitheatre and making their way towards the boxes, Mrs. Appleby spied several acquaintances on the far side and immediately excused herself.

"You go ahead with the gels, my lord, and never worry your head about me. I'll find my way to you as soon as I've had a word or two with Clara Lewes and dear Lady Meadhead," she said, shooing them ahead of her and turning in the opposite direction.

James did not try to dissuade her. He knew it was beyond his powers to bring the woman to a sense of her responsibility, but it disturbed him that Mrs. Appleby was willing to leave two beautiful young ladies to the care of a gentleman she'd known scarce above an hour. So much for Lady Trevelyan's prudence in providing Serena with a suitable chaperon, he thought, shepherding the girls to a box.

He got them comfortably settled and was looking for Mrs. Appleby when Serena suddenly clutched his arm, drawing his attention to the parade of six matched ponies and riders entering the ring.

They trotted in perfect unison and formed a neat line in front of the boxes of spectators. At a signal from the lead rider, the ponies flexed their forelegs and appeared to bow to the audience. Serena clapped her hands with unfeigned delight and craned her neck to watch as they cantered to the far side of the arena to repeat the manoeuvre.

The crowd applauded and the equestrians waved briefly before turning their mounts—all except the smallest of the riders, astride the last pony. He stayed where he was, waving his hat wildly and grinning broadly at the crowd. Several voices shouted to him, and at last he looked round and noticed the others had ridden off. He wheeled his mount and urged it after them, kicking and shouting, but to no avail. The small black pony refused to budge, and there were loud titters of amusement from the audience.

The rider dismounted, scurried in front of the creature and stood tugging at the ribbons. When the pony still refused to move, he dropped the reins, ran round behind the beast and pushed at the creature's withers. The pony suddenly galloped forward and the small clown fell flat on his face.

Mrs. Appleby rejoined James and the girls just as the impish figure scrambled up and raced after his mount—while the other ponies, having circled round the arena, came up fast behind him. A collective gasp rose from the crowd as the nimble-footed clown seemed to trip and fall directly in front of the racing ponies.

James missed seeing what occurred next. Mrs. Appleby halted immediately in front of him and stood transfixed until the clown rolled free in a neat somersault and came to his feet unharmed.

"Well, did you ever see the like?" she asked, finally taking her seat next to her daughter.

James refrained from remarking that he had not been able to see anything and instead politely enquired if his guests desired refreshments. His offer was declined, the young ladies being too enthralled by the emergence of three splendid white stallions on either side of the arena.

Mrs. Appleby leaned across Cressida and nudged James. "Do not look now, my lord, but I do believe the lady directly across the way is trying to gain your attention. The blonde over there sitting beside Rotterdam—though what he might be doing here has me in a puzzle, for this is not his sort of entertainment. She has been staring in our direction since I arrived, however, and I am most certain she is not one of *my* acquaintances."

James looked in the direction indicated and was astonished to see Mrs. Beryl Tallant seated in the box opposite. He recognized the Brenermans behind her, and with a surge of anger, Lord Rotterdam lounging in a chair at her side. Beryl sent him a warm smile and waved a lacy handkerchief. James nodded curtly in return. He knew her appearance here could not be mere coincidence, for he had told Beryl of his plans, and he found himself annoyed that she had followed him.

He was even more angry that she had included Rotterdam in her party. It was beyond forgiveness, in fact. Beryl knew his opinion of that gentleman, and particularly his own desire to shield Serena from the scoundrel's attention, which had given rise to so much unfortunate gossip. If Beryl's intent had been to arouse his jealousy, she had erred badly. He was out of temper, uncomfortable, and entirely too conscious of Serena sitting beside him, her hands folded modestly and her eyes downcast.

Serena had heard Mrs. Appleby's remarks. Indeed, nearly everyone in their section had heard the lady's comments, for her voice carried remarkably. She recognized Mrs. Tallant instantly and did not miss the intimate look the widow exchanged with Jamie. Serena glanced down at once, studying her gloved fingers and fighting her disappointment.

She would not cry, she told herself fiercely, twisting her hands tightly together. She *would not*. But the notion that Jamie was so enamoured of the widow he could not bear to be apart from her, not even for one afternoon, engulfed her in a cloud of despair. It never occurred to her that Jamie had not arranged the assignation, for it was inconceivable that Mrs. Tallant would have followed him of her own accord.

If James and Serena were less than enthused, Cressida was elated. She, never having seen Mrs. Tallant, had not the least notion who the lady might be, and did not care. All her attention was focused on Rotterdam, and she could barely contain her excitement. Never would she have believed she would meet the cynical rake in such a simple place as Astley's, and she viewed his presence as a wonderful Heaven-sent opportunity.

Cressy made certain her mother was still engaged in conversation with the lady in the adjoining box, and took a deep breath. Striving to sound nonchalant, she spoke to James, "We must all stroll round and allow you the opportunity to say hello to your friends at the intermission. I declare it is always so pleasant when one chances to meet an acquaintance unexpectedly."

James did not reply and Serena took his silence for agreement. She wondered if there was some way she could avoid the meeting, for at the moment she did not feel she could behave civilly to the widow. Cressy, she knew, would devote all her attention to Rotterdam, and Jamie, no doubt, would behave most gallantly to Mrs. Tallant. Serena would be left feeling decidedly *de trop*. Blinking rapidly, she pretended absorption in the antics of a trio of clowns, but the whirling figures blurred before her. She clapped when the audience did, though she'd not the least notion of what she was applauding. She swallowed the lump in her throat and quietly asked Jamie if he would procure a glass of lemonade for her.

When he was gone, she leaned towards her friend and whispered, "The lady across the way is Mrs. Tallant. Cressy, you must help me to avoid meeting her."

"Not Jamie's widow?" Her friend's wide blue eyes assessed the lady anew, and though she did not wish Serena ill, she fervently hoped the woman did indeed have her sights set on Jamie and not Lord Rotterdam. She was formidable competition and cut just the sort of sophisticated figure to which Miss Appleby aspired.

"Will you help me, Cressy?"

Her friend nodded. She was fond of Serena and quite understood her misery, but still she could not possibly forgo the chance of speaking with Rotterdam. She angled for a compromise. "You must feign a headache, my dear, which should not be hard, for you look as though you are suffering a megrim. Just stay in the box with Mama, and I shall walk round with Lynton and see what the lady is about."

There was no time to say more. James was returning with their drinks, and they settled back to watch the last act before intermission. Serena doubted Jamie would be deceived by so obvious a ploy. Doubtless he would think it a childish effort on her part to keep him from Mrs. Tallant's side. Oh, why did the widow have to come and spoil everything?

Serena moved slightly apart from Jamie, but she could not concentrate on the pantomime before them. Her throat ached and her mouth was abnormally dry. She lifted her glass to take a sip of lemonade, but it slipped from her nervous fingers and shattered on the floor. The sweet drink splashed over her dress, as well as Jamie's pantaloons and glossy boots. Serena stared in horror, embarrassed beyond measure.

"What the devil?" James cried, rising abruptly to his feet and wiping futilely at the spreading stain. "Serena, my dear, are you all right?"

She turned a stricken face up to him. "Oh, Jamie, I am so sorry. It was dreadfully clumsy of me, but the glass just slipped from my hand."

"Never mind that—you are not hurt, are you? The glass did not cut you?"

"No, but I've ruined your clothes!"

"It's nothing," he assured her with a forgiving smile. "And Cecil will be thankful you at least spared my coat. But what of your dress? Stand up, Serena, and see if you can blot it a bit."

Mrs. Appleby had risen and shouldered Jamie aside. With a comforting arm about Serena's waist, she drew the girl to the rear of the box. "Don't be embarrassed, child. Such a mishap could happen to anyone," she said, offering Serena a clean handkerchief. "Here, my dear, brush it off with this before the stain has time to set."

Cressida peered over her mother's shoulder, a huge grin turning up the corners of her mouth. She had not thought Serena so clever. This certainly would prevent her friend from leaving the box.

Mrs. Appleby examined the damage and declared it was not so bad after all. "You must have your maid boil up a handful of fig leaves, my dear, and when it is reduced, dip a sponge into the liquid and rub it over the stain. I promise you, it will remove every trace and your pretty dress will be as good as new."

"Thank you, Mrs. Appleby," Serena murmured, promising to remember, but it was small consolation to her at present. Her dressed looked a sight with a large, ugly stain down the centre. Jamie must think her the clumsiest wretch alive.

"May we be of assistance?" a cool voice asked from the doorway, and Beryl Tallant stepped into the box, followed by Lord Rotterdam. "We saw the commotion from across the way and wondered if there had been an accident of some sort."

Serena took one look at the elegantly clad Mrs. Tallant and devoutly wished there was somewhere she might hide, but Mrs. Appleby proved equal to the occasion. Sweeping forward, she shielded Serena from view and addressed the widow. "How very kind of you, but I do not believe we have been introduced. Are you a friend of Miss Trevelyan's?"

Beryl blushed slightly and glanced at James. "We are acquainted, and I am very well known to Lord Lynton."

"Indeed?" Mrs. Appleby murmured, managing to convey with one word that she doubted such a thing was possible. She turned questioning eyes to James.

He reluctantly performed the introductions and could not help but be conscious of the ladies' coolness towards Beryl. Though they said everything proper, it was abundantly clear they did not welcome the widow.

Beryl appeared impervious to their snubs, and after making Lord Rotterdam known to the group, enquired how best she could help. "Such an unfortunate occurrence, my dear. Doubtless you will not wish to remain in that damp dress, for the afternoon breeze can be frightfully chilly."

"I am certain it will quickly dry," Cressy said, her eyes on Rotterdam's tall form. They simply could not leave now. "You would not wish to miss the other exhibitions, would you, Serena?"

"I should not like to spoil the afternoon for the rest of you," Serena agreed quietly, though her dearest desire was to leave at once.

Mrs. Tallant strongly advised against her remaining and was immediately drawn into an argument with Mrs. Appleby. Cressy, of course, took her mother's side, and James was helplessly caught in the middle, trying to keep peace.

Rotterdam took the opportunity to step close to Serena and smile down at her. "It appears you are among cats, my little mouse. My driver and carriage are without—should you like me to rescue you?"

Serena glanced at Jamie, but it appeared in his zeal to defend Mrs. Tallant, he had forgotten her own existence. She looked up at Rotterdam and saw nothing but gentle compassion and understanding in his green eyes. His sympathy brought her close to tears and the notion of escaping was tremendously tempting. Still, she hesitated and asked softly, "But what of Mrs. Tallant, my lord?"

"I believe she will be well looked after until I return, but it is of no import. At present, my only concern is for you. Allow me to arrange matters, my dear." He linked her arm through his. "Shall we?"

Serena remained where she was, watching Jamie for a moment. She would have given anything to hear him say those words, to be first in his concern, but he was still hovering beside the widow, apparently defending her from Mrs. Appleby's pointed remarks. She suddenly felt an overwhelming impulse to leave, an irresistible urge to show Jamie she would not be treated so shabbily. Heeding her inner voice, she turned to Rotterdam and nodded, allowing him to lead her towards the door. It seemed to Serena that everyone noticed them at once, and as questions were hurled at them, she looked down at her feet. Rotterdam's calm voice overrode the others.

"The question is settled, so please do not concern yourselves. I shall drive Miss Trevelyan to her home and the rest of you may stay and enjoy the exhibition."

"My lord, surely you do not mean to desert me?" the widow demanded, and only Rotterdam caught the gleam of triumph in her eyes.

"If Serena goes, I am leaving as well," Cressy cried, stepping next to her friend.

"If anyone sees Serena home, it will be myself," James announced with a challenging, angry look at Rotterdam.

"Please," Serena cried in real anguish. "I cannot bear to hear you all arguing so. My lord, may we leave now?"

Silence descended as the group fell back, slightly ashamed of their bickering.

Rotterdam opened the door for her and glanced back at James. "You may entrust her to my care, Lynton. You have my word I will see her safely home. Mrs. Tallant, I shall return within the hour, though I shall quite understand if you do not desire to wait. Good day, ladies."

"JAMES IS A FOOL and he has botched this affair," Cuthbert muttered angrily to Eleazar from his place at the back of the box. "It serves him right to see Serena walk off with Rotterdam."

"He is not the only fool," Eleazar warned quietly. "And if you do not cease your infernal interference, both you and Serena will reap the consequences."

"What? I have done nothing—"

"Except convince Serena to leave with Rotterdam. Had you left her alone, she and James would have resolved this."

"Ha! How can you say so with the widow scheming before our eyes? My poor little Serena," Cuthbert said, shaking his head. He felt her heartache as though it were his own. "I begin to think James is not worthy of my girl and she would do well to forget him."

"Her happiness lies with him," Eleazar cautioned. "You have seen the charts—a wrong choice now and she will live a life of misery. Is that truly what you wish for Serena?"

"No, but what ought we to do?" Cuthbert demanded, frustrated by his inability to help. "Everything has gone awry."

Eleazar felt a surge of affection for the crusty little major and wished he could do more to ease his way through this last, troublesome stage. But Cuthbert had to earn his wings on his own, just as Serena and James would have to find their own destiny. He sighed and offered what advice he could. "Help Serena to keep her faith in James. She must believe in him or all will be lost."

"Easy for you to say," Cuthbert replied tartly, watching his beloved charge leave with Rotterdam. "And what of *him?*"

"I did warn you that if you stirred a hornets' nest, someone might get stung."

CHAPTER NINE

ROTTERDAM WAS as good as his word. He whisked Serena from the amphitheatre with a minimum of fuss. His driver, warned always to be on the alert for his master, appeared quickly, and Serena soon found herself seated in a comfortable, well-sprung open carriage. The bright sunshine did as much to warm her body as her spirit, and after a quarter of a mile, she remembered her manners and managed to thank the earl for coming to her aid.

"It appears to be my destiny," he murmured, watching her profile and admiring the way the sun shot coppery lights through her dark hair.

"I beg your pardon?" Serena said, glancing up at him in some confusion.

Rotterdam smiled. "Rescuing you is becoming a habit, Miss Trevelyan. First it was from that set of tabbies my sister collects. Confess you were bored to tears," he teased, hoping to coax a smile from her.

"Not in the least," she replied, making an effort to respond to his raillery. "I will own your presence certainly enlivened the morning, but not that it in any way constituted a rescue."

Her smile wavered and did not quite reach her eyes, but it did have the effect of restoring some colour to her pale cheeks, and he was encouraged to provoke her further.

"Very well," he agreed with an amused laugh. "But what of Mrs. Hertford's masquerade? Will you not admit you stood in need of a champion and owe me a debt of gratitude for sending old Crawford about his business?"

Serena could not look at him. She stared mutely at the driver's broad back, recalling a faint impression of the tall gentleman in the black domino who had freed her from the grasping hands of the drunkard. She dimly remembered he had called the man "Crawford."

"Come, Miss Trevelyan," he taunted lightly. "A game of cat-and-mouse is hardly entertaining if the mouse will not play. You have several choices, you know. You might thank me profusely for coming to your rescue, or beg me prettily not to reveal my knowledge of your presence in such a house...or even call my bluff and pretend you have no notion of what I am referring to."

"What is it you want of me, my lord?" Serena asked quietly.

Her dark eyes had a haunted look and he instantly regretted his words. She was too inexperienced to answer him in kind, as he had intended. His own smile faded and he spoke abruptly. "My apologies, Miss Trevelyan, for an ill-chosen jest. It was not my intention to alarm you but merely to tease you into better spirits. Whatever secrets you harbour are safe with me. I give you my word as a gentleman."

"A gentleman would never have mentioned the matter, my lord," she reproved him, but her voice was gentle and she added softly, "But if you spoke the truth, then I do indeed owe you a debt of gratitude. Dare I ask how I might repay you?"

"There are plenty who would be quick to advise you not to place yourself in my debt, Miss Trevelyan."

"Perhaps they are ill-acquainted with you, my lord?" she returned, and this time her smile did not waver.

"Thank you, my dear, but though I wish I might claim otherwise, you would do well to heed their advice. I fear I do not always adhere to the code of polite behaviour gentlemen like Lynton set such store by."

"Jamie—Lord Lynton—has very high standards," Serena said, utterly unaware of the way her eyes sparkled at the mere mention of his name, or of the note of pride in her voice.

"I gather your acquaintance with him is of long standing?"

Serena nodded. "From the cradle. Lord Lynton's lands adjoin my father's and we grew up together."

"Allow me to give you one bit of advice, my girl. It is not altogether wise to wear your heart upon your sleeve for all the world to see."

Serena turned her head. The words were not unkindly said and were even lacking Rotterdam's usual sarcastic inflection, but she could have faced him better had he mocked her. It was the pity in his eyes she could not bear.

She pretended an inordinate interest in the passing houses and then remarked with apparent unconcern, "If you are referring to Lord Lynton, I must tell you, sir, that I do indeed adore him." She laughed lightly and added, "He is the brother I never had and the one gentleman I must always hold in affection."

Rotterdam raised his heavy brows, his scepticism plain. "I have previously admired your honesty, Miss Trevelyan, and yet you now choose to repay your debt by prevaricating with me. I am disappointed, my dear."

"I am sure I do not know what you mean," she said, flushing at his rebuke.

"No? Then allow me to elaborate. I suspect the *affection* you profess for Lynton has very little to do with sisterly feelings, and you do me an injustice if you think I would swallow such a taradiddle."

"Very well, then," she replied sharply, facing him squarely now, her eyes flashing with anger. "I love Jamie. I always have and I always shall. Does that please you, my lord? Does it afford you amusement?"

"Not at all," he answered with unruffled calm. "But at least you are answering honestly, and little though you may think it, my intention was not to hurt you. I was contemplating the future. Tell me, Miss Trevelyan, what will you do if your gallant weds the lovely widow?"

His question left her bereft of words and she turned away from his probing eyes. She wanted to cry that such a thing was not possible, but he had voiced the fear she carried deep within her heart. Doubt shook her faith and for a long moment she could not reply.

She struggled for composure, aware of his catlike eyes observing her. "This is a most improper conversation, my lord. I cannot think it right to discuss Lord Lynton or Mrs. Tallant in such a manner."

"Most improper," he agreed, "but then I warned you I do not subscribe to a gentlemanly code of behaviour. Still, 'tis not idle gossip, my dear, or mere curiosity, and I should like an answer. An honest answer, if you will, to cancel the debt of gratitude you owe me."

"I shall go on loving him," she said defiantly, raising her chin and clenching her hands to hide their sudden trembling. "Doubtless you have never given your heart to anyone or you would understand that, once given, it cannot so easily be recalled. If I should never see Jamie again, I would go on loving him till the day I die."

This time it was Rotterdam who glanced away. The carriage was turning into Manchester Square, and as the horses slowed, he remarked gently, "Lynton is a remarkably fortunate man. I wonder if he realizes it."

Serena mistrusted his words and glared at him, but there was no derision in his voice, no trace of scorn in his eyes.

He watched her, smiling at her disbelief. "It *was* a compliment, Miss Trevelyan, but do not trouble to answer. Now, I have kept my pledge and returned you safely home. Shall I see you in, or will it occasion too many elaborate explanations?"

"Inasmuch as Mama is at the window and has seen you arrive, I fear the explanations cannot be avoided," she replied with a tired sigh. Realizing how ungrateful she must sound, she smiled and laid a hand on his arm. "Do come in, my lord. Mama will be pleased to welcome you."

ACROSS TOWN, in the neat little house on Chesterfield Street, James was having his own share of troubles. Beryl had dismissed her maid in order that they might speak privately, but it was very soon clear the widow was determined to misunderstand every word he spoke. He accepted the sherry she offered only to placate her.

"I cannot stay long—" he began.

"Really?" she interrupted, her voice laced with irony. "I quite thought we had an engagement this evening."

"We do, of course, but there are matters to which I must attend. Surely you can understand that?" he added.

Beryl turned her back to him and crossed the room to stand before the window. She glanced over her shoulder, taunting him. "Oh, I understand well enough, my lord. You must run off and see for yourself that little Miss Trevelyan arrived safely home."

"That sort of remark is unworthy of you, Beryl," James replied quietly, coming up behind her. "Serena was entrusted to my care and I should never have allowed her to leave with Rotterdam. Her name has already been linked with his. To be seen driving with him will make her the subject of every gossip-monger in Town."

"Very touching, my lord, but I hardly think such concern is warranted. Why can you not accept that Rotterdam means her no harm?" she asked, turning to face him.

"I do not trust the man, and as I recall, I confided as much to you," James replied stiffly, his own temper rising. "Though, of course, I was not aware you were so well acquainted. Why did you invite him today, Beryl? You knew my feelings."

"Perhaps to test those feelings," she murmured, watching him closely. "I was disturbed when you spoke so vehemently of him. I have known Ivor for years and he is not the rogue you paint him."

"And yet you saw no need to mention your friendship?"

"Not when you were so agitated at the mere mention of his name! I feared being painted with the same brush. A lady in my position must tread warily, for I have not the protection of a noble name or family to ensure my respectability."

"I see," James replied. "You could not mention your acquaintance with him to me, but did not hesitate to appear in public on his arm. Your actions are hardly consistent, my dear.''

Beryl looked down at her hands and her voice trembled slightly. ''I thought if you became better acquainted with him, you would realize your mistake. And if you were not so blind with jealousy, you would also realize that should Rotterdam offer for Miss Trevelyan, it would be an excellent match.''

''Offer for her? It is you who are blind. I only wish I may live to see him do anything so honourable.''

Beryl took both his hands in her own and looked up at him. ''Listen to yourself, James. You will not even grant him the benefit of the doubt. No, hear me out. Ivor may have carried on numerous affairs, but to my knowledge he has *never* bestowed his attentions on a young girl of respectable birth.''

''That is not to say there may not be a first time.''

Beryl's eyes filled with tears again and she let his hands go, twisting away from him. ''You are too enamoured of her to see the truth. Too jealous to see her wed another, even though it would be to her advantage.''

James placed his hands on her shoulders and turned her to face him. ''I wish I could convince you that you are mistaken. I would gladly see Serena wed a gentleman she cares for and who cares for her. I simply do not believe Rotterdam is that gentleman.''

''No, nor any other,'' she answered sadly. ''Your behaviour this afternoon proved that well enough. Let me go, James. You run along to Miss Trevelyan. It is clear that is where your preference lies, and I have not your talent for deceiving myself.''

He released her, sighing in frustration. "Very well. Perhaps you will be in a more rational mood this evening. I shall call for you at eight."

"No, James. Under the circumstances I cannot think it wise to see you again. You are free to devote all your time to Miss Trevelyan," she said, holding her breath and praying that she had gambled correctly.

"Beryl, this is madness. You cannot be serious."

"Oh, but I am. Though you tried to hide it, I saw your agitation when the Brenermans left me stranded. It was obvious you resented the necessity of driving me home. Well, I will not place you in such a position again."

"I do not believe this," he replied, striding to the sideboard and refilling his glass. The sherry splashed against the mahogany table but, in his anger, he hardly noticed. "I will admit I was enraged, but you must own I had cause. What with Miss Appleby creating a scene and her mother behaving as though I had planned the entire affair, it was enough to try a saint's patience. 'Twas fortunate their friends offered to see them home when Mrs. Appleby had the brass to refuse to ride in the same carriage as you. Of course I was furious. Would you have had me accept such an insult to you with complacency?"

"I wish I might believe you, James. With all my heart I wish it, but in the carriage all you spoke of was your fear that Mrs. Appleby would spread the tale about, and the harm it would do Miss Trevelyan—"

"I explained that. For Serena to be seen driving with Rotterdam will occasion a great deal of talk and I—"

"So you said, James. Repeatedly. Your concern for her far outweighed any care you might have had for my feelings," she answered softly. She blinked her eyes and a teardrop fell against her white cheek. She made no move to check it but lifted her head, her blue eyes awash with tears. "I envy her, you know."

"You have no need, I swear," he cried, touched by her vulnerability and moving to take her in his arms. "Beryl, my dear, I—"

"I've brought your tea, Mrs. Tallant," Mildred interrupted noisily, backing into the room with an ornate tray and service.

Startled by the sound of the maid's voice, James stepped away from the widow and swung round. He missed the look of scathing anger on Beryl's face, but the maid saw it and the tray shook in her hands. James went to her assistance at once and, removing the heavy tray, set it firmly on the serving table.

Mildred mumbled an apology and quickly backed from the room, but the spell had been broken.

James remained standing near the door, but he smiled across at Beryl. "I had not realized it was so late. If we are to attend the theatre this evening, I must go home and change." He hesitated, his hand on the door. "Will you grant me leave?"

Beryl knew the opportunity had been lost and now was not the time to press her ultimatum. She silently cursed her maid's ill timing, but managed to cast a bereft look at James and reply in a small, forlorn voice, "It is probably most unwise of me, but I find I can refuse you nothing when you look at me in just that way."

"I shall make it a point to remember that," he said with a half smile. "Eight o'clock, then?"

Beryl nodded, holding her temper in check until he left. Then she rang for her maid.

Mildred stepped in timidly, dropped a swift curtsy, and stood with her head down, twisting her hands together.

"You are never, *never*, to intrude when I am with Lord Lynton. If I want you, I shall ring for you. Is that quite clear?"

"Yes, ma'am. I won't do it again, ma'am. 'Twas only you said before as how I weren't to leave you alone and I thought—"

"That was before, you stupid girl. Now leave me," she ordered, her beautiful face distorted with fury. She barely restrained an impulse to throw something at the maid. She had been so close to bringing Lynton to the point of making an offer. Every instinct told her that in another moment he would have proposed, had not Mildred interrupted.

Now she would have to depend on Rotterdam. She'd deliberately sought out the earl that morning and laughingly taunted him over the rumours of his supposed attraction to Miss Trevelyan, recklessly wagering a hundred pounds he could not win the girl away from Lynton.

Rotterdam had not risen to the bait, but she'd told him of her plans to visit Astley's and that Miss Trevelyan would be present, if he dared put his infamous charm to the test.

He had agreed readily enough, but Beryl recalled uneasily that he had neither accepted nor rejected her wager. She half suspected he had accompanied her merely to find out what motive she'd had for proposing the wager. His success in walking off with the girl from beneath Lynton's nose was something she had not anticipated. Dear Ivor. It would be well worth a hundred pounds if he succeeded, she thought, for surely his actions signalled his compliance. Yes, well worth it, even if it meant selling her emerald ring.

LORD LYNTON LEFT the widow and absent-mindedly made the journey to Lady Marcham's house. His first order of business must be to make certain Serena had arrived safely home, but Beryl had given him much to consider, and his thoughts were considerably disordered. Such was his confusion that it was several minutes before he realized the carriage had stopped and the driver was impatiently waiting for him to alight. He paid the man off, and only then did it occur to him that he did not know what to say to Lady Trevelyan. If Serena had not returned . . .

A footman opened the door to him and James enquired for Miss Trevelyan.

Pritchard appeared behind the footman and informed him the family was all at tea. "Are they expecting you, my lord?"

"Not precisely, but if you will take my card in, I believe Miss Trevelyan will wish to see me."

"Very good, my lord. Would you step into the small salon?"

James waited impatiently, pacing the room, though it was hardly above five minutes before the butler returned. "If you will follow me, my lord?" he asked, and led the way to the sitting-room. He announced Lord Lynton at the door and discreetly withdrew.

James stared at the intimate scene before him. He was barely aware of Lord Marcham, standing next to his wife's chair, or of Lady Trevelyan, sitting opposite in the tall wing chair. His attention was all on Serena, sitting next to Rotterdam on the sofa.

She had changed her dress for a pretty blue muslin with capped sleeves and had let down her hair, the dark waves falling below her shoulders and small tendrils curling about her ears and brow. It was a simple style, but he thought it suited her. Indeed, he thought she had never looked more lovely. Her dark eyes seemed to sparkle, and when he'd entered, she had been laughing at something Rotterdam had said—her lips curving in a delightful smile and her head tilted slightly back, exposing the slender column of her throat.

Then Lord Marcham was striding forward to greet him, his arm outstretched and his mouth creased in a wide grin. "Ah, Lynton. I rather thought we might see you this afternoon. Come in, come in. We're having a bit of a celebration. The doctor has allowed my wife to join us for the first time since her illness."

James made his bow to Lady Marcham, congratulated her on her recovery, and apologized for intruding. She was kindness itself, however, insisting she was delighted to meet him at last. Much to her sister's surprise, she directed Sylvester to draw up a chair for the young man next to herself and asked Marjorie to pour him a cup of tea.

James accepted gratefully. He had not met with much kindness that day, and after a rather cool welcome from Lady Trevelyan, he was doubly thankful for the warm sympathy in Lady Marcham's eyes.

She tried to draw him out, asking questions about his recent visit abroad. Jamie answered dutifully, but his attention was elsewhere, and twice he had to beg pardon and ask her to repeat her question. Louisa smiled to herself, watching his eyes stray once again to the sofa where Serena was engaged in a low-voiced conversation with Rotterdam.

Serena, after her first flush of pleasure at hearing Jamie had arrived, had greeted him rather shyly and then returned to her conversation with Rotterdam. She was still embarrassed by the afternoon's fiasco and deeply hurt that Jamie had abandoned her in favour of the widow. She willed herself not to look at him, but she was very much aware of his presence. She tried to attend to the nonsensical story Rotterdam was telling, but her ears were attuned to the sound of Jamie's voice.

"Come back, Miss Trevelyan," Rotterdam murmured, recapturing her attention. "Remember that bit of advice I gave you, mouse. 'Tis not wise to show your emotions so clearly."

Serena used her fan to cool her suddenly warm cheeks. "I am sure I do not know what you mean, sir."

"Excellent," he whispered. "Let him think you indifferent. It will do more good than gazing at him with your heart in your eyes."

"I would not stoop to such tactics, my lord," she whispered furiously.

"If true, you are the first lady I have known who would not."

"You must know some very peculiar people, sir," she returned. "Although I believe you did say Mrs. Tallant is a friend of yours?"

Rotterdam threw back his head and laughed aloud. "Wonderful, my dear. There is hope for you after all, and now I think it would be wise to take my leave." He stood and, over the protests of Lady Trevelyan and Lord Marcham, insisted he must go.

Lady Trevelyan rose and extended her hand. "I must thank you, my lord, for your care of my daughter."

"All gratitude must be on my side. This has been most enjoyable and I hope you will allow me the privilege of repaying your hospitality. Will you and your lovely daughter consent to be my guests at the opera on Tuesday evening next? And Lord and Lady Marcham, of course. It will be just a small party, but quite informal, and I hope to persuade my sister, Lady Colchester, to join us.''

"We should be honoured, my lord," Marjorie replied at once, favouring him with a warm smile. "Allow me to walk with you to the door.''

James heard the exchange with a mixture of astonishment and disbelief. Had he been wrong about Rotterdam? Was it possible the man was pursuing Serena with honourable intentions? Appearing at the opera house as Serena's escort, in company with his elder sister, was akin to making a public proclamation of his intentions. He stared after the earl and was only recalled to the present by Lady Marcham's gentle touch.

"I hope you will not think it ill-mannered of me, Lord Lynton, but much as I enjoy your conversation, I should now like a word with my husband. Will you be good enough to allow him your seat? And I think perhaps my niece would like a word with you.''

James saw the understanding in her brown eyes and, rising gracefully, bowed over her hand. "It has been a very great pleasure to meet you, Lady Marcham, and I stand indebted to you.''

"Nonsense. Be off with you," she scolded, and with a wave of her hand, brought Sylvester to her side.

James took her at her word and quickly moved to the sofa where Serena was seated. She had her head down as she sipped her tea, and he wondered for a moment if she were angry with him. "May I join you?" he asked hesitantly.

She glanced up at him, saw the troubled look in his eyes, and smiled. "Of course, Jamie."

He was aware of Lady Marcham speaking softly to her husband and kept his own voice pitched low as he sat down beside Serena. "I really came to apologize, but I will readily understand if you find my conduct this afternoon unforgivable."

Serena lowered her eyes, but not before James had seen the hurt mirrored there. Still, she did not reproach him, but whispered quietly, "Thank you, but no apology is necessary. I—I only regret embarrassing you in front of your friend."

"If you think that, little one, then I did, indeed, behave badly, and would fully deserve it if you were never to speak to me again."

Serena glanced up, meeting his remorseful eyes, and her heart was suddenly lighter. "Well, that would be most unpleasant for me," she replied, her dimples peeping out. "Besides, Jamie, I know you had Cressy and Mrs. Appleby to attend to, which cannot have been easy."

"An understatement. Was your mother very angry?"

"At first, perhaps," she answered, her hand unconsciously caressing the rim of her cup. "But Lord Rotterdam stayed for tea, and he explained how it all came about and made everything right with Mama."

"He behaved civilly towards you? You must tell me if he did not," James said, a hard note creeping into his voice.

"Of course he did," she replied, pleased at his concern but knowing intuitively it would not do to tell Jamie the things Rotterdam had said. She was a little flustered and hurriedly added, "Really, he is a charm-

ing gentleman and I am certain no lady could ask for a
more considerate escort. I wish you could have been
here, Jamie, and heard the funny stories he told. I vow
he is prodigiously amusing!''

Serena paused to sip her tea and did not notice the
stricken look on Jamie's face.

He recovered quickly, however, and smiled down at
her. ''Well, I am glad to hear it, and judging by the rapt
attention he was paying you, it seems your admiration
for the gentleman is returned. Unless I am much mistaken, you have made a conquest, minx, and will soon
be the envy of every young lady in London.''

''Jamie! What nonsense you talk—just because Lord
Rotterdam stayed for tea,'' she replied, blushing furiously.

''Mmm. Only wait till after you are seen at the opera
with him. All the tabbies' tongues will be wagging. You
will be so popular, I dare say I shall have to stand in line
just for a word with you.''

His tone was teasing, but there was a note of serious-
ness in his voice and a strange, almost wounded look in
his eyes that shook Serena to the depths of her soul. She
reached for his hand, his name on her lips, but Lady
Trevelyan chose that moment to return and James rose
smoothly to his feet. He never saw the forlorn little
gesture.

''CAN YOU NOT do something?'' Cuthbert demanded,
hovering behind the sofa where Serena and James were
seated. He watched dismally as James rose to take his
leave.

''What would you suggest?'' Eleazar replied a trifle
testily. ''A bolt of lightning?''

"It wouldn't hurt! Good heavens, what a botch they've made of it. He thinks Serena *cares* for Rotterdam. Could you not have made him look at her there at the last? Her heart was in her eyes for all the world to see."

"I told you we cannot interfere. The rules—"

"Rules! Is that all you can think of? This is no time for scruples, not with Serena's happiness at stake! We cannot just stand idly by and do nothing. I'll be damned if I will!"

A bolt of lightning lit the sky outside and a thunderous wind blew, bending the trees nearly double. Even the windows shook. "Careful, Cuthbert," Eleazar warned, glancing uneasily about. "You may be just that."

"Perhaps I spoke a bit hastily," he muttered. "But Eleazar, it cannot be meant for things to come to such an end. Surely there must be something we can do?"

"I believe you have done quite enough," Eleazar said with a sigh. "Leave them be." The major had not yet learned the value of patience or the futility of fighting Destiny. Although it was much to Cuthbert's credit that he cared so deeply, it was also due to his interference that Serena had been pitchforked into Rotterdam's company, tangling all their affairs. Still, it was difficult not to feel a trifle sorry for Cuthbert.

James, however, was near the door and duty called. "I must go," Eleazar murmured, adding with a measure of kindness, "Do not despair, old friend. The game is not yet played. Only, Cuthbert—remember there are no guarantees. No matter what we might wish for our charges, the final choice must be theirs alone."

CHAPTER TEN

JAMES LEFT the Marcham residence in a daze and headed back to his rooms.

He had been a fool. He knew it; had realized it with blinding clarity the instant he'd seen Serena sitting beside Rotterdam, her dark head bent close to the earl's. The intimate murmur of their conversation had grated against his ears, and he had turned away lest he give in to the overwhelming desire to remove the rake by the seat of his breeches. Nor had the gnawing ache inside him eased with the knowledge that Rotterdam's intentions appeared to be honourable.

Beryl had been right all along. He laughed aloud at the irony of it, a harsh bark of a laugh that made Paddy turn to stare at him. James abruptly ordered him to take him to White's instead, a glimmer of an idea beginning to surface. Beryl would understand, he thought. She'd suspected his heart belonged to Serena and had complained of being jealous. It was the truth, though he had been foolish enough to deny it. But if he owned it now, admitted how deeply he cared for Serena, surely Beryl would not wish to receive an offer from him. There were other men who found her attractive. Dozens. She could have her pick of any of them, he reasoned.

He strode into White's with a lightened heart, believing there was hope after all. Once free of his entanglement with the widow, he could court Serena, sweep her off her feet in the manner she deserved, and prove to her she belonged to him in a way she never could to Rotterdam.

"Well, if it ain't Lynton," a deep voice boomed from one of the card-tables.

James glanced round and saw Edward Kendrick at a table with Ormond and Selwyn. He nodded and strolled over, loath to talk just then but too polite to give his friends the go-by. Empty glasses stood in front of each of them, and James, judging by their bloodshot eyes and lopsided grins, guessed it was not the first round the trio had enjoyed.

The red-headed Ormond stared up at him. "The widow let you off the leash tonight? We had not looked to see you here, but you're a welcome sight. Sit down, Lynton, sit down."

"I cannot stay long," James answered, remaining on his feet. "As it happens, I do have an engagement later this evening."

Kendrick nodded knowingly. "It's getting to be a blasted habit," he complained, shuffling the cards. "Every time we get a decent fourth for a game, the fellow ups and gets married. Don't know what the world's coming to. Ormond, order us another round of drinks."

"Have you offered for her yet, Lynton?" Selwyn demanded, his words slightly slurred. "I've a wager on with Chichester. Ten to one, they're giving at Boodle's."

"I beg your pardon?" James said, a growing uneasiness creeping over him.

"Ten to one you'll offer for the widow before the month's out," Selwyn obligingly explained. "Let me know when I can collect."

Ormond kicked him under the table and Selwyn yelped, leaning over to rub his foot.

Lord Ormond smiled apologetically at James. "Sorry, old man. Hardly sporting to put you on the spot, but you must know the word is out the black wid—er, Mrs. Tallant means to have you."

James, making a supreme effort, grinned down at Selwyn and spoke with an affability he was far from feeling. "I shouldn't count your winnings yet. The lady in question has dozens of suitors."

Selwyn snorted rudely. "None with a pretty title and a tidy fortune at hand. She'd be a fool to pass you by."

Ormond suffered a fit of coughing, and there was an uncomfortable second of silence before he and Kendrick both began speaking at once of inconsequential matters. When Selwyn opened his mouth and received yet another hefty kick in the shin, he loudly demanded to know if Ormond had run mad.

James smiled, though his heart was in his boots. He remained, talking idly, for another few moments and then took his leave. He made his way upstairs and found a deserted nook where he could drink in peace. But not even the straight whisky he downed could dull the ache in his heart. He cursed himself for a blind fool and tried desperately to think of a way to mend matters, knowing all the while there was none.

Selwyn had made two things clear to him. He had led the world to believe he would offer for Beryl, and was therefore honour-bound to do so. No gentleman would raise the expectations of a lady and then draw back. *Bad ton,* he muttered into his glass. And for all that Selwyn had been in his cups, he was right about the gentlemen who clustered about Beryl. None had a title or commanded a fortune to match his own. With sudden insight, James realized there was only a very slim chance the widow would refuse his offer.

EVEN THAT TINY SLIVER of hope was extinguished in the week that followed. Beryl was all sweetness, enquiring with solicitous concern for Serena as though they had never argued. She apologized prettily for what she termed her unreasonable behaviour and had stood on tiptoe to kiss James on the cheek. "It is only that you matter such a great deal to me," she'd whispered. "I could not bear it were I to lose you now."

It left him with nothing to say.

The following Friday James escorted the widow, along with Angela and George Brenerman, to the theatre in Bow Street. They arrived early and had just taken their seats in a box to the left of the stage when there was a stir in the audience. James glanced at the boxes opposite, where a party was just arriving. It was Rotterdam, with Serena at his side looking exceptionally lovely in a white gown that sparkled in the light and set off her beautiful shoulders. He watched with bitter envy as the earl seated her beside him and then turned to speak to Lady Trevelyan. Rotterdam's sister, Lady Colchester, was present, which no doubt accounted for the murmurs of excitement and craned necks of the rest of the theatre-goers.

Beryl touched his arm and leaned towards him. "Your little Serena looks quite beautiful. She will make a splendid countess, do you not think?"

James agreed morosely and tore his gaze away from Serena. It was too painful to watch her with Rotterdam. He tried to focus his attention on Beryl, but when she turned to speak to Angela, he found himself again staring at Serena, willing her to look at him.

As if in answer, she lifted her head and glanced in his direction. Their eyes met across the crowded, noisy room, and for a brief instant there was no one else present. She smiled, almost hesitantly, and just slightly inclined her head, her lips moving silently.

"Hello, Jamie."

He could almost hear the words and stirred in his seat, longing to go to her. But then Rotterdam drew her attention, leaning possessively towards her, and James saw her laughing at something he said. Jealousy tore at him and he longed for the satisfaction of meeting Rotterdam on the duelling field. He'd run his sword through those broad shoulders and wipe the devilish grin from the earl's face.

Beryl, watching the emotions fly across his face, judged the moment right. "James, my dear, I had a letter from my uncle this morning. He will be arriving in Town next week and is most anxious to meet you."

"Your uncle?"

"Yes, Uncle Richard. I did tell you he is my only kinsman, and, well, I suppose he feels it is his duty to speak with you." She played with her fan, peering up at him over the furled edge. "I have written to him so often about you, I fear he means to ask your intentions."

He had been expecting such an announcement, but it still came as something of a shock and he could think of nothing to say. He glanced again at Serena, but her attention was all for Rotterdam.

"He wishes us to dine with him on Monday," Beryl said, laying her hand against his arm. "Is that agreeable with you?"

James heard the catch in her voice, and caught a glimpse of something in her eyes. Fear? Was she afraid, even now with Serena nearly betrothed, that he'd not do

the honourable thing? Poor Beryl. None of this was her
fault, and she deserved better. James vowed he would
do his best for her, but at the moment he could not bear
to look at her. He nodded and, with his eyes deter-
minedly fixed on the stage, whispered, "Monday will be
fine."

LADY TREVELYAN HAD NOTED the wistful look her
daughter cast at young Lynton at the theatre, but dis-
counted it as part of her childish infatuation. She truly
believed Serena to be happy and well on the way to becoming the future Countess of Rotterdam. She herself
was in alt and never tired of discussing her daughter's
good fortune in attracting the earl, and had even been
moved to write to her husband that he might very well
anticipate a call from Lord Rotterdam. She felt there
was little doubt an offer would be forthcoming, since
Lady Colchester, that highest of sticklers, had been
moved to give the match her tacit approval. Everyone
expected an announcement. Even Cressy had refused to
speak to Serena, accusing her friend of setting her cap
for Rotterdam.

Serena, feeling much as though her world was falling apart, sent Cressida an apologetic appeal, begging
for a private word. To her surprise, Cressy sent back a
friendly note suggesting they drive in the park as usual
on Tuesday. She appeared in unusually good spirits that
day and when Serena tried to speak of Rotterdam,
Cressy airily brushed her apologies aside.

"It is of no concern of mine if you choose to wed
Rotterdam, though I think he'll make a dreadful husband."

Serena looked at her searchingly, but Cressy seemed sincere, and she murmured, "I believed you to be set on Rotterdam. This is a sudden change of heart, is it not?"

Cressida laughed. "It is, indeed, but hardly unusual. Only consider yourself, my dear. When we first met, all you could speak of was Jamie, and now everyone is saying you will wed Rotterdam."

"I hate all the gossip," Serena said, a trace of sadness in her voice.

But Cressy did not hear her. She'd turned to wave at a pair of scarlet-clad soldiers and, when they had passed, said softly, "There is something delightfully enticing about a uniform, have you noticed?"

Serena saw the brightness in her friend's eyes and the gentle blush suffusing her cheeks, and she suddenly understood Cressy's abrupt change of heart. "Who is he?"

"Captain Stewart," Cressy owned with downcast eyes, suddenly shy. "He has called several times, and he took me driving yesterday. Oh, Serena, I think...I think I may be in love."

"I am so glad for you," Serena said, holding her hand tightly. "But what of Rotterdam? Are you certain, my dear?"

"Quite. He was just an infatuation. You are welcome to him, Serena."

But I don't want him. Serena didn't say the words aloud, and she listened patiently to Cressy extolling the many virtues of Captain Stewart. She was truly glad for her friend, and it even encouraged her a little. If Cressy, who'd been so devoted to Rotterdam, could find happiness with someone else, perhaps one day she could, too.

ONLY LADY MARCHAM had dared to express the opinion that on occasion she thought her niece looked a trifle melancholy. The notion had quickly been ridiculed by her sister as nonsensical, and Louisa had put it from her mind. In truth, she was too preoccupied with her husband to give Serena more than a passing thought. Since her illness, Sylvester had been the most adoring of husbands, and their marriage had taken on a new intimacy. Louisa now appeared in the mornings with becoming colour in her cheeks, and she fairly glowed whenever Sylvester entered the room. For his part, it seemed he could not resist any excuse to pass close to his wife's chair and touch her hand or caress her shoulder.

His loving demonstrations to Louisa were so apparent that Marjorie was drawn to tease her sister. As they were sitting in the drawing-room late one afternoon, she remarked, "I believe this is the first time we have been alone since your illness. Perhaps Serena and I should cut our visit short, for I vow I feel much as though we are intruding on a newly wed couple!"

Louisa blushed but did not deny the charge. She confided, "Is it not wonderful? Oh, Marjorie, for years I have agonized, believing Sylvester must wish for a wife who could give him an heir, but he has made me realize that it does not matter to him."

"I seem to recall Lady Fitzhugh telling you something of the sort," her sister replied with a smile.

Louisa nodded. "But that is not the same as Sylvester telling me. You will not repeat this, I know, but when I was so ill, he told me he would not wish to live if I did not recover. He said life would have no meaning for him without me by his side."

Marjorie laughed at her, though not unkindly. "You do indeed sound like a bride, my dear, and I am most glad for you. I only hope my Serena will be as happily wed. They do say rakes, once reformed, make the best of husbands, and I must say Lord Rotterdam has shown her every consideration. He is taking her driving today, you know."

As if on cue, Pritchard tapped on the door and entered. "Beggin' your pardon, my lady, but Lord Rotterdam has arrived."

"Oh, splendid," Lady Trevelyan answered, setting down her cup and adjusting the ruffled cap she wore. "Do show him in, Pritchard, and please send Mary up to tell Miss Serena."

"Very well, my lady."

Serena, however, was already aware of Rotterdam's arrival. She had heard his carriage approach and, gazing out the window, had watched the earl enter the house. It seemed to her it was not so long ago she'd stood at the same window and watched Jamie arrive. It was a pity, she thought, that the sight of Rotterdam did not fill her with the same sort of elation she'd felt then. She turned listlessly from the window, listening as Annie thanked Mary and assured her Miss Serena would be down shortly. She straightened her shoulders, put all thoughts of Jamie from her mind, and prepared to show the world a light-hearted countenance. As Rotterdam had said, it would not do to wear her heart on her sleeve.

Annie shut the door firmly and faced her mistress. She was perhaps the only person who knew how truly unhappy Serena was, and she longed to help, but there was nothing she could do save see her young lady was properly and becomingly clothed.

"Well, he's here, miss," she said, her voice unusually brisk to hide her sympathy. "Let me help you into your pelisse, and don't be arguing with me. For all the sun's shining a bit, there's a chill in the air, and I expect we're in for a storm."

"Thank you, Annie," Serena said, dutifully submitting to being buttoned into the coatlike garment that matched her lilac walking dress. It was in the latest style, trimmed with heavy ornamental black braid, and Annie assured her she'd never looked more lovely.

Rotterdam agreed when he saw her and complimented Serena on her excellent taste. "Madame Dusante's?" he enquired with a knowledgeable lift of one brow.

"Indeed it is, my lord, and how amazing you should recognize her handiwork," Serena answered with a smile.

"Not at all, my dear," he replied with a wicked grin. "My sister patronizes her establishment."

Rotterdam refused the tea, apologizing to the ladies but explaining he was anxious to leave, for he had a new team of horses he was trying and hated to keep them standing overly long. Serena laughed, but did not keep him waiting. She kissed her aunt and mother, and knowing they planned to visit Lady Fitzhugh, asked to be remembered to her.

"So you have made the acquaintance of Maria," Rotterdam commented, escorting her out. "I am most curious to know what you thought of her."

"I found her completely delightful," she said as he handed her into the carriage. "Indeed, of all the ladies I have met in London, Lady Fitzhugh is the one I most admire."

"Another example of your excellent taste," he said, giving the nod to his tiger to stand away from the horses' heads. "She is an original spirit and one of the wisest ladies I know."

"That is high praise indeed, for you know so many, my lord," Serena murmured.

"Wretched girl! Did no one ever teach you proper respect for your elders?"

"Papa," Serena began with a solemn air that was belied by the mischievous look in her eyes, "always said one should not be accorded respect merely because of age or circumstance, but should earn it by one's conduct and wisdom."

"Why do I feel it is fortunate for me your papa remained in the country?" he asked, glancing across at her.

"I am sure you would like each other," Serena said, thinking of her father with sudden longing. He would know how to advise her.

Rotterdam caught the slight trace of sadness in her voice, but he said nothing until he had safely guided the horses through the gate at Hyde Park and then slowed their pace. "I hope you are right, mouse. I should like to meet your papa and put a certain question before him."

"My lord, I—"

"I thought we agreed you would address me as Ivor?"

"No, my lord, we did not. You suggested it and I said—"

"Your papa would not approve," he finished for her. "Do not remind me. You have a great many admirable qualities, my dear, but your facility for recalling every word ever spoken to you is, at times, extremely annoying."

"I am sorry, my lord, but you did say there should be only honesty between us," Serena said, returning a wave from Lord Ormond, whose carriage was approaching.

"There! That is precisely the sort of thing I mean," Rotterdam answered, and completely ignoring Ormond, who clearly wished to stop and exchange a few words, he stepped up his horses' pace. He gave the go-by to Lady Hardwicke, who raised a tentative hand in greeting, and only a curt nod in answer to Sally Jersey's imperative wave. "This park is becoming damnably crowded of late."

"Inasmuch as you do not bother to acknowledge anyone, I should not think it would trouble you."

"It would not if my only intention was to idle away an hour or two, but I wish a word with you in private." He turned onto a narrow, seldom-used path and, when it appeared free of carriages, drew his team to a smooth halt. He glanced over his shoulder at his tiger and curtly instructed the young man to inspect the shrubbery some dozen feet away.

"My lord, I do not think—"

"Hush, my dear. You know you stand in no danger from me." He waited until his tiger was out of hearing and then turned to her. He had to smile as he looked at her, for she sat primly, her gloved hands neatly folded in her lap and her head slightly bowed. A cool breeze blew a stray curl softly against her cheek. Rotterdam reached out and smoothed it back.

"Serena, look at me," he commanded, and with his hand gently lifted her chin. "You are surely not afraid of me?"

"No, my lord, only of what you might say," she replied softly, her immense eyes silently pleading with him.

"I had hoped your sentiments might have undergone a change this past week. You have enjoyed yourself, have you not?"

She nodded and reached up to hold his hand with her own. "You are a wonderful friend, my lord, and I know I should be...honoured that you have spent so much time with me, but—"

"You do realize Lynton has all but offered for the widow?" he interrupted. "It can only be a matter of time before the engagement is announced," he said, his thumb lightly caressing hers. He saw her long lashes sweep down, hiding for a second the anguish in her eyes. "Serena, I realize how you must feel, but I think, given time, you might come to care for me in the same way. I will not press you, though if you would allow me leave to call on your father—"

"Please, Ivor, do not," she interrupted. "I wish I might believe my feelings would change, but I know they will not." She shook her head, turning away from him. "It was wrong of me to accept your invitations when I knew people were talking about us, but I thought...I believed you understood."

"I do, but a man cannot be blamed for hoping, mouse," he said lightly, while silently cursing the fates that had led him to become enamoured of the one young lady who could not return his regard. What had started as a game with him, partly on an impulse to confound the widow and partly to teach young Lynton a lesson, had turned into something much more serious than he'd bargained for.

He sighed. Serena looked so forlorn that he longed to sweep her into his arms and kiss away her heartache, but he knew it was not his kisses she yearned for and there was nothing he could do but make the way as easy as possible for her.

He smiled down at her. "I suppose it was my natural conceit that led me to believe no young lady could fail to find me irresistibly charming did I but choose to exert myself," he began in a teasing voice.

"An understandable failing, my lord, when there are legions of ladies who do adore you," she answered, blinking rapidly to guard against the onset of sudden tears.

"Then I shall apply to you for a list," he said, signalling for his tiger to return.

"It would take me days to compose it," she replied with a smile. "There are so many who think you top-of-the-trees, though I fear a word from you would frighten half of them."

"My abominable conceit again. I was not aware I frightened innocent young ladies. Have I *any* admirable qualities?"

"Dozens," she answered, smiling warmly at him.

They passed the remainder of the drive in perfect charity with each other, and the light-hearted banter between them did much to restore Serena's composure. They arrived in Manchester Square just as large raindrops were beginning to splatter the pavement, and Rotterdam hurried her to the door. Pritchard was waiting and had it open as they approached and the rain began to fall in earnest. He waited patiently to accept the earl's hat and cape, but Rotterdam shook his head.

"But will you not stay at least until the rain abates?" Serena asked, concerned.

"Thank you, my dear, but there are a number of things I must attend to, having suddenly recollected an engagement out of Town. I charge you to make my apologies to your mama and Lady Marcham."

"My lord, you are not leaving because I—"

"Now who is abominably conceited? You have nothing to do with it, Miss Mouse, and were you not such an innocent I would tell you about the charms of a certain young lady in the wilds of Yorkshire. Suffice it to say that *she* holds I am without fault and is anxiously waiting, even as we speak, for my return."

Serena, conscious of the butler and footman waiting just a few steps away, smiled and extended her hand. "Then I shall not detain you, my lord, but may we hope to see you on your return?"

"You may depend on it, my dear. As you have pointed out, I have many faults, but slighting my friends is not among them—and I hope we shall always be friends."

"Thank you, Ivor," she said, so softly Pritchard could not hear. She remained at the door, watching as he bounded down the steps and ran for his carriage. She could barely see him for the rain, or perhaps because of the unshed tears that blurred her vision.

Pritchard stepped forward. "Excuse me, Miss Serena, but there is a matter that I feel I should bring to your attention."

Serena swallowed over the tightness of her throat. "Allow me a few moments to put off my hat and cloak, and then I shall speak with you," she promised, hurrying towards the stairs.

She tried to untie the strings of her bonnet as she climbed the steps, but they had been dampened by the rain and her fingers seemed unusually clumsy. She opened the door to her bedchamber, calling for Annie, but the maid was not in the room.

Serena pulled off the pelisse and then, sitting at the small dressing-table, worked at untangling the bonnet strings. Annie had still not appeared when she finally succeeded in removing it, and she pulled the bell rope to summon her. What she needed, she decided, was a bracing cup of tea before she went down and faced Mama.

She knew her mother would be disappointed when she learned Serena would not be receiving an offer from Lord Rotterdam. Perhaps she would even wish to return to Malmesbury at once, Serena thought, taking some small comfort from the idea of going home to Papa.

There was a gentle tap on the door and Serena called for Annie to come in, but it was Mary who stepped into the room and enquired politely if she might be of service.

"Thank you. I only wished for a cup of tea, but where is Annie?"

Mary stood awkwardly, staring at a spot on the wall above Serena's head. "She is not here anymore, miss."

"I beg your pardon?" Serena said, quite certain she had not heard correctly.

"She was turned off just this afternoon, miss, and Mrs. Moppit said as 'ow I was to wait on you."

"I do not understand this," Serena said, rising and crossing the room. "Look at me, Mary. What has happened to Annie?"

"Oh, miss, it was dreadful, and I didn't want to be the one to tell you. Annie was crying something fierce and said she didn't do it, but Mrs. Moppit found the pearls in her bag and she made Pritchard come and look. There weren't nothing no one could do, miss."

"Take a deep breath, Mary, and calm yourself. What pearls are you talking about?"

"Lady Marcham's necklace. Thomas was to take it to the jewellers today to fix it 'cause the clasp is loose, but when Etta went up to get it, it was gone, miss. Mrs. Moppit was in a rare taking and she turned the house upside down searching for it and then they found it—in Annie's bag."

"I see," Serena said slowly. "And what did my aunt say?"

"She wasn't here, miss, nor your mama either. They went out in the carriage and ain't come back yet. Poor Annie, miss, she swore she never saw them pearls before."

"Tell Mrs. Moppit I shall be down directly. I should like to see her, and also Pritchard, Thomas and Etta in the drawing-room."

"Yes, miss," Mary replied nervously, and dropped a curtsy.

That must have been what Pritchard had tried to tell her, Serena thought, pacing the room. She would stake her life that Annie was not a thief. This was all Mrs. Moppit's doing, of that she was certain. The woman had abused Annie from the beginning and disliked it intensely when Serena had dared interfere.

A flash of lightning lit the room and Serena glanced at the pouring rain. Where had Annie gone? She knew the girl had been raised at an orphanage. She had no relatives, no one to turn to. Serena doubted she even had enough pocket money to hire a carriage to take her back to the home. She must find her.

Serena sat down at the mahogany desk and hastily scribbled two notes. Blotting them carefully, she slipped them into her pocket. Then, gathering up her pelisse and bonnet, she hurried down to the drawing-room. The staff was waiting for her.

Etta looked tearful and Pritchard and Thomas anxious to be of help, but Mrs. Moppit faced her with a sullen, resentful look on her doughy face, and it was she who stepped forward. "Mary said you wished to see us, miss, and I expect it's about that maid. I knew from the minute I laid eyes on that girl she was no good, and I was right. A common thief she was, and I'll not have that sort working in the house."

Serena looked at her for a long moment until the woman nervously glanced away. "I do not believe Annie ever took anything that did not belong to her. At present, I—"

"It was found in her bag," the housekeeper insisted stubbornly.

"At present," Serena repeated, "all I wish to do is find her. Do any of you know where she might have gone?"

"She set off north, Miss Serena, is all I can tell you," Thomas said.

Pritchard shook his head and lifted his hands helplessly. "The maids are under the supervision of the housekeeper, miss."

"What of you, Etta? Do you know where she went on her half days?" Serena asked.

"This is foolishness," Mrs. Moppit declared, folding her arms over her chest. "All this fuss over a thief, and keeping us from our work. I don't think Lady Marcham will—"

"You may leave us, Mrs. Moppit," Serena interrupted. "Though I am certain my aunt will have a great deal to say to you when she returns."

"Well! If that is all the thanks I get for trying to protect my lady's jewels, then I'll not be saying another word except I don't doubt the day will come when you'll regret this, miss." Giving Serena a venomous glare, she marched from the room with her head held high.

Serena ignored her. "Etta? Do you know of any friends Annie had? Anyone she might have visited?"

"I'm sorry, Miss Serena, but she never stepped out much and she never talked about no one."

"All right, Etta, you may go. Thomas, be so good as to deliver this note to Lord Lynton at once," she directed, withdrawing one of the notes from her pocket and handing it to him with several pound notes. "Hire a carriage, and if his lordship is not at home, return here as quickly as possible. Keep the carriage waiting, for I shall need it."

"You will surely not search for her yourself, Miss Serena?" Pritchard asked as soon as the footman had left.

"I must," she murmured distractedly. "I am certain Annie did not take my aunt's pearls, and to think of her being turned out in this storm without any money or any place to go... Papa would say it is my duty."

"But surely when Lady Marcham or my lord returns, they can attend to this. Your aunt will not like you going out in the storm."

"I hope they return before I leave, but if not, you will give this note to my aunt," she replied, drawing out the second sheet of paper.

"Yes, miss," he said, reluctantly accepting the scrap, and then hesitantly added, "Is there anything I can do?"

Serena sighed and sank into the sofa cushions. "Perhaps you could ask Mary to bring me a cup of tea," she suggested with a ghost of a smile. "I did not quite like to ask Mrs. Moppit."

"I will arrange it at once," he replied, and left the room with a determined air.

Time dragged slowly, and as each minute passed, the storm seemed to intensify. Branches knocked against the windows of the drawing-room, and the rumble of thunder drowned out any hope of hearing a carriage arrive. Thoughts of Annie out in the storm alone, without food or money and probably soaked to the skin, plagued Serena. She barely noticed Mary slip in with her tea or the footman Pritchard sent to build up the fire.

When the clock on the mantel stood at half past six, she rose restlessly, nearly convinced Thomas had become lost or had been unable to hire a carriage. She would give him five more minutes, she thought, and then ask Pritchard to send another footman to engage a carriage for her. Three minutes had passed when Thomas rushed in.

"His lordship's coming, miss," he gasped. "He's following in his own carriage and should be here in a few moments." His breath came in ragged bursts and Serena realized the man was drenched.

"Thank you, Thomas," she said, gathering her gloves and bonnet. "I pray you will not have caught cold. Do go get into some dry clothes."

Serena stepped out into the hall. Pritchard was near the door and glanced round as he heard her approach. "He's just turning in the square, miss."

"I shall go out to him."

"I rather thought you would, miss. If you will allow me," he said, unfurling a large black umbrella as he opened the door. He held it over her, struggling to keep pace as she ran for the carriage. James had not time to alight, and seeing Serena, he threw open the door and reached down a hand to her.

"Jamie!" she cried, and impulsively embraced him.

For an instant, his arms tightened about her. Then, remembering the impropriety of such behaviour, James released her and looked down into her face. "All right, minx, suppose you tell me what this is all about?"

CUTHBERT HURRIED after her and settled beside Eleazar on top of the carriage. "I wish you would do something about this dreadful weather. I suppose James may be trusted to see she comes to no harm," he said.

"You can depend upon it," Eleazar answered.

"Then perhaps some good will come of this. It is rather like the old days when they were always rushing off to rescue some poor creature or other."

"Frequently at your instigation."

Cuthbert nodded. "It drew them together then, and I suspect it will do so now. Did you see how he embraced her? You said the choice must be theirs. Well, it's obvious that if left alone, they'd choose each other."

"Indeed," Eleazar agreed sadly. "But you are forgetting that James is not in a position to choose. There is still the widow."

"Oh, damn—drat the widow," Cuthbert amended as lightning rippled round them and thunder rocked the sky.

CHAPTER ELEVEN

SERENA, her hands warm between Jamie's, looked up at him with large, trusting eyes. "I shall tell you everything, but you must first direct Paddy to drive us to Guilford Street—to the Foundling Hospital there—and we must hurry."

When he hesitated, she begged him. "Please, Jamie—the matter is urgent."

"I will take you wherever you wish, of course, but it seems a strange place to visit at this hour." However, the desperate look in her eyes persuaded him, and he leaned out the window and ordered Paddy to drive them to the hospital.

"Oh, thank you," she said with a sigh, sinking back against the cushioned seat.

"*Mmm*. Now, would you please explain why we must go there in the middle of a storm? What mischief have you been brewing, little one?"

"Oh, Jamie, it is the most dreadful thing," Serena began, and quickly explained what had occurred. "So you see," she finished a few moments later, "it is the only place I could think where Annie might have gone. I have been praying we shall find her there."

"Well, we shall soon know," Jamie said, and squeezed her hand as the carriage came to a halt. The gates were barred to traffic and it was some time before a young boy answered their summons. They could hear

Paddy announcing that Viscount Lynton and Miss Trevelyan, niece to the Earl of Marcham, had urgent business within.

The lad seemed impervious to reason or rank and stubbornly insisted the hospital was closed to visitors. James motioned for Serena to remain in the carriage while he climbed out and dealt with the lad. A couple of shillings was all it took to induce the boy to unlock the gates, but in those few moments, James was soaked to the skin. He climbed back into the carriage, shivering slightly.

Paddy drew up as close to the doors as was possible, and James helped Serena down, protecting her from the strong winds and blowing rain as much as he could, but she, too, was drenched by the time an elderly woman in a neat black bombazine uniform opened the door.

"My stars!" she cried. "Come in, come in at once." She stepped back and a gust of wind slammed the door open. Jamie caught it and shut it tightly after them.

The matron, who identified herself as Mrs. Lambert, eyed them warily until James produced his calling card and introduced Serena. Her first impression—that this was another unwed mother seeking a place for her infant—was quickly revised as she motioned them to follow her into a warm, brightly lit sitting-room.

"Now, my lady, my lord, what may I do for you? The hospital is closed to visitors just now, but if I may be of assistance in some way?"

Serena thought the woman had a compassionate face and she stretched out a hand in entreaty. "Thank you for admitting us, and please believe I would not impose on you were the matter not serious. Can you tell me if you have ever had a young girl here by the name of Annie Phelps? She has, until today, been in the employ of my aunt, Lady Marcham.''

"Oh dear, has something happened to her? I was so sure she would do well. Such a biddable girl and Lady Marcham so kind.''

"She was turned off, but it was a dreadful mistake and I am trying to find her. Mrs. Lambert, do you know whether Annie had any family or friends she might go to if she were in trouble?''

"No, miss. Annie was left here as a babe. She has no family that I know of and I don't recollect her having any close friends. Annie kept to herself, like.''

"I see. Well, at least there is a chance Annie might return here, and if you would permit me, I should like to wait for a while.''

"Why, certainly. I was about to suggest you might wish to remain here until the storm lessens. It is a terrible night to be out, is it not? Now, is there anything you would like? A cup of tea, perhaps?''

Serena shook her head. "Nothing, thank you. But would you please let the boy tending the gate know that Annie is expected?''

"Of course, my dear, I shall attend to it at once.''

She left them alone and Serena turned to James with a shaky smile. "It *is* a terrible night, and I can imagine what Cecil would say to me for dragging you out into such a storm!''

"I seem to remember more than one occasion when we were out in worse," James reminded her. "Sit down, Serena, and tell me how long you intend to wait.''

"I...do not know. An hour or two? I haven't any notion how long it might take to walk here from my aunt's.''

James had drawn out his watch. "Nor do I, but I should think if she left this afternoon, she would be here by nine at the latest, even if she had to rest occasionally and seek shelter from the storm. It is half past seven now."

"Unless . . . Jamie, do you think it possible she was already here and was turned away at the gate?"

He shook his head as he returned the watch to his pocket. "No, I questioned the boy about that. Apparently, we are the only ones foolish enough to venture out in the storm."

He paced restlessly about the room and Serena, watching him, sensed there was something troubling him. When he drew out his watch for the second time, she was certain of it. "Jamie? If you have another engagement, you must not scruple to leave me here. The matron can arrange a carriage for me, and when Annie comes, I shall have her to lend me countenance."

If Annie comes, he thought silently, but could not depress her hopes by voicing his doubts aloud. He crossed the room and sat down beside her. "Do not concern yourself, little one. I do have plans, but nothing so urgent it will not keep."

"With Mrs. Tallant?" she asked, looking down at her hands. When he did not reply, she added softly, "Then you must go."

James heard the slight quiver in her voice and asked himself how they had ever come to this pass. Aloud he said, "I was just thinking of sending a message to her. I am sure she will understand—"

"I think it would be best if you went yourself, Jamie," she interrupted.

He saw the stubborn set of her chin and knew there would be no arguing with her. "Very well, but promise you will wait here for me. After I explain what has occurred, I shall return for you and Annie. It should not take me long.''

"Of course, Jamie," Serena replied, making every effort to hide her disappointment. "It is an excellent scheme, and you must make my apologies to Mrs. Tallant for spoiling her evening.''

"There is no need for you to apologize. This is far more important than a mere dinner engagement," he said with a wry smile as he rose. "Are you quite sure you will not be nervous waiting here alone?''

"Now you are being foolish. I shall ring for Mrs. Lambert and ask if she will join me for a cup of tea. Doubtless, I shall be a great deal more comfortable than you will be out in that terrible storm. Do have a care, Jamie.''

"I shall, and I'll be back before you have time to miss me.''

There was always sufficient time to miss him, Serena thought, watching his tall figure go out the door. It seemed to her that he took all the warmth of the room with him.

JAMES HATED LEAVING Serena alone, but he could not, in good conscience, fail to keep his engagement with the widow. In truth, he did not at all mind missing an evening with the Brenermans, and had been absurdly pleased when Serena had sent for him. He knew, however, that Beryl would be exceedingly angry. She might have been understanding and sympathetic had it been anyone else, but she would not take kindly to her plans being cancelled for Serena's sake. James sought words with which to placate her as the carriage barrelled along, and was near to convincing himself Beryl would not wish to go out on such an evening in any case. Although his carriage was sturdily built, the wind buffeted it, rocking it precariously. He gave thanks Paddy had the reins, for he knew no better whip.

His trust was not misplaced. Paddy got them safely to Chesterfield Street, and sooner than James had anticipated. He climbed out, shouted to Paddy he'd return as quickly as possible, and hunching his shoulders against the wind, made his way to Beryl's gate.

The iron grille was not fastened, but swung wildly on its hinges, and James carefully shut it before making his way up the walk. The wind was not as strong here, for the house faced west and was sheltered from the worst of it, though the rain still fell in torrents. James, with his head down, did not notice at first that the front door was ajar—not until he lifted the knocker and the door swung inwards.

"Beryl?" he called, stepping inside, but his voice was lost in a loud roll of thunder. He shut the door firmly, imagining Milly must not have closed it securely and the wind had blown it off the latch. He unfastened his cape, sodden with rain, and left it to drip in the entry, then made his way towards the drawing-room. The hall was only dimly lit and he was more preoccupied with being careful not to trip over a table or chair than with making his presence known.

He was near the door of the drawing-room when he heard Beryl's lilting laughter, followed by the sound of a deep masculine voice. He recognized it at once as belonging to George Brenerman. James wondered what the man was doing there early and cursed his bad luck. He had not anticipated having to make his apologies in the presence of anyone else. He smothered his annoyance and was about to call out to Beryl when the sense of her words penetrated his mind. He paused where he was, his hand on the doorknob.

Her voice came to him clearly. "George, darling, you must be reasonable about this. You know I adore you, but I can ill afford to take any chances until I am safely wed. Now, do run along, my sweet. James will be here soon and I must change my gown."

"Lynton! That's all I hear from you. I believe you have become overly fond of him. I am asking you— begging you—to give it up, Beryl, and come with me to America. I'd have a chance to make something of myself there, and I swear you'd not regret it."

"I told you, George, I cannot bear to live in genteel poverty. Do not pout, my love. When I am wed there will be ample time for us to be together. I doubt James will be a possessive husband, and he has told me he means to spend a year or two at that place of his in the country, so I dare say he will not mind if I visit London or Paris alone."

"And I am to wait about until you have time to see me, is that it?"

"Please, dearest, I cannot argue with you now. You agreed to be sensible about this, and you know I cannot bear it when you are angry with me...."

The words trailed off and only the soft rustle of silk could be heard. James swung the door open. Although he had expected to find the widow in Brenerman's arms, the sight of them embracing nevertheless shocked him. Beryl's duplicity and the humiliation of being taken for a fool filled him with a burning anger, but as he stood silently watching the pair, his fury was tempered by an overwhelming sense of relief.

He coughed politely. The couple sprang guiltily apart and he leaned casually against the door. "Pray forgive the untimely intrusion, my dear."

"James!" Beryl cried, and made to move towards him, but he stayed her with one out-thrust arm.

"I came to tell you that I could not keep our engagement this evening, but it appears you also have a prior commitment."

"James, I can explain if you will only allow me the chance," she pleaded, tears filling her pretty blue eyes. "I know how it must look—"

"I believe I have heard sufficient to render your explanations unnecessary," he interrupted. "Rude of me to eavesdrop, of course, but I have been in the hall for several moments."

"You—you heard our conversation?" she asked, closing her eyes.

"Everything. But do not look so troubled, my dear. I suspect it is fortunate for both our sakes that I stumbled upon this touching little scene." Anger laced his voice as he added, "It appears we were both mistaken in each other. I may have been a fool, but I would never be the complacent sort of husband you envisioned."

Her face whitened and she seemed to stumble. George caught her and drew her to him. Beryl hid her face against his shoulder and he spoke to James over her head. "I am glad you heard, Lynton. I never liked deceiving you. Now, if you don't object, I should like to be alone with Beryl. If you wish to meet me—"

"Call you out?" James asked with an incredulous grin. "Not at all. I wish you nothing but good fortune." He straightened and gazed at the widow, who was sobbing gently against Brenerman's shoulder. "I have the feeling you will have need of it. Good night, George."

He made his way back down the hall and encountered Mildred who was lingering at the foot of the stairs, a frightened look on her pale face. "My lord! I never heard the knocker," she stammered. "Did you see madam?"

"I did," he replied drily, swinging the wet cape about his shoulders. "Tell her I hope she has a pleasant voyage."

"Voyage, my lord?"

"Indeed, yes. I fancy your mistress is even now planning a trip to America. I hope you have a fondness for sailing, Milly."

James left her staring at him in open-mouthed amazement and dashed for his carriage, his spirits soaring. What he felt most was a pressing anxiety to return to Serena.

Paddy was waiting, and as soon as he saw his master's booted foot safely within the door, he whipped up the horses. The rain seemed to have abated somewhat and they made excellent time back to the hospital, but for all his efforts, they were not quick enough.

The lad at the entrance was on the watch for them, but instead of swinging open the gate, he called up to Paddy, "The young lady's left. She said to tell his lordship she's taking Annie home."

James heard and stuck his head out the window, fighting his disappointment. "How long ago did she leave?"

The boy shrugged. "Ten minutes maybe. I flagged a hackney and Matron saw her and the girl off."

James tossed the lad a coin and called up to his driver, "Take us home, Paddy." The man needed no further urging, and the carriage lurched forward.

James settled back. For all his impatience to see Serena, he must first get Paddy home. The rain had nearly stopped, but there was a sharp, biting wind and he knew his driver must be chilled to the bone. He'd give strict orders for Paddy to get into dry clothes and have a bite to eat before going straight to bed. For once, the man would have to let someone else attend to the horses.

As he expected, Paddy put up an argument, but James remained adamant, and after dismissing his driver, he took the steps two at a time, his mind racing ahead. He could change, flag a carriage and be with Serena within the hour. It would be late for a call, of course, but he was certain that under the circumstances Lady Trevelyan would forgive him.

Caesar was waiting for him, stretched across the door, and James grinned down at him as he opened it. "At least you have enough sense to come in out of the rain."

"Which is more than I can say for some," Cecil scolded, coming to take his lordship's sopping cape and hat. "It is not a fit night for anyone to be about. Man or beast," he added, warily keeping an eye on Caesar.

"I agree," James said with a cheerful grin. "But duty calls, and I am only stopping long enough to change my clothes. Have I a clean coat?"

Cecil nodded, but his face was grave. "You got my message, then?"

James stripped off his coat and glanced up. "No, what message?"

"I sent word to Mrs. Tallant's. Lady Lynton is in Town and wishes to see you at once."

"Mother? Good heavens! When did she arrive and where is she staying? Never tell me she's opened the Town house!"

Cecil handed him a folded note. "The footman said she arrived with Sir Laurence Trevelyan and she's visiting Lady Marcham."

James scanned the scrawled note, apparently written in some agitation. He had difficulty deciphering the lines, but it appeared Sir Laurence had driven to Town in anticipation of Serena receiving an offer from Rotterdam. Lady Lynton wrote she found such news distressing, as did "dear Sir Laurence," and she could not understand what James was about. "Surely it had always been understood that he and Serena would make a match of it?" The note ran on in that vein, but he paid scant attention to the rest of it.

How like his mother to suddenly champion Serena, he thought, tossing the note aside and striding quickly towards the bedchamber to change his coat. Cecil followed to assist him, but James ordered him to see that the carriage was brought round at once.

"Yes, my lord. Paddy—"

"Not a word to Paddy. I'll drive myself and take young Timothy with me. Hurry, Cecil. There's no time to be lost."

BY THE TIME James returned to Manchester Square, it was almost ten o'clock. It was far too late for a call, but James had the excuse of his mother's arrival, and he was determined to see Serena no matter what the hour. He tossed the reins to Timothy and sprang from the carriage with an urgency that boded ill for anyone who stood in his way.

To his surprise, he found the house still brightly lit and his impatient knock quickly answered by a footman. Not waiting for an invitation, James shouldered his way inside and demanded to see Miss Trevelyan. The footman was considerably startled and about to protest when Pritchard materialized. After welcoming James more warmly than was his custom, the butler led him down the long hall to the green drawing-room. From the sounds within, James feared Serena's betrothal was already being celebrated.

Pritchard announced him and he stepped slowly forward, his gaze raking the room. His first thought was one of relief that Rotterdam was not present, and then he forgot everything else as Serena came to meet him, her hands outstretched in greeting.

"Jamie, I knew you would come and I must apologize for not waiting for you at the hospital, but Annie was dreadfully sick and I thought it best to get her home at once."

"Of course," he said, smiling down at her. She was so dear to him . . . her piquant face, her large eyes, the sweetness of her smile. He had been a fool not to realize it sooner.

"Jamie? You look so odd. Is something wrong?"

"It depends," he murmured, keeping a tight hold on her hands. "Serena, may we speak privately? There is so much I have to tell you."

Jamie looked so troubled she longed to step into his arms and smooth away the worried frown between his eyes. But she was also aware of the others waiting— waiting and watching.

He saw her hesitation and added persuasively, "Please, my dear—I know it is late, but I came as quickly as I could to see you."

"To see me?" Her heart turned over at his words and she sought to lighten the tension between them with a laugh. "Do not, I beg you, tell your mama that," she whispered. "She has been expecting you any time this past hour. Come and say hello. Afterwards, I am sure we can manage a few moments alone."

"Then let us not keep her waiting," James replied, and with Serena by his side, crossed the room to make his filial bow to his mother. He bent, kissed her warmly, and expressed his surprise at seeing her in London.

"*Humph.* You left me little choice, James, since you chose not to answer my letters."

"But I did . . ." he began, and flushed guiltily as he recalled his mother's last letter, left on the table a fortnight ago, lost somewhere beneath a pile of newspapers.

Sir Laurence laughed. "I gather you write with the same frequency as Serena, and poor Henrietta has all my sympathy. Just wait till you have children of your own and they neglect you. Then you both will understand what a difficult burden we parents bear." He gazed fondly at his daughter, expecting her to protest. When she did not answer at all, he chuckled softly. "Serena? Are you listening, my dear?"

Serena had not heard the question, but she finally realized her father was staring at her, apparently waiting for some sort of reply, and she glanced about in helpless confusion.

Louisa, always perceptive, came to her rescue. "I have no doubt my niece wrote you, Laurence, and doubtless you will find her letters somewhere on my husband's desk, still waiting for a frank."

"I knew somehow I would take the blame in all this," Lord Marcham said, and lifted a decanter in James's direction. "A glass of brandy, Lynton? We are celebrating a great many good tidings tonight."

Here it comes, James thought, bracing himself. He hid his turbulent thoughts behind a façade of politeness and nodded at Marcham. "Thank you, sir, I don't mind if I do. The weather was a bit inclement this evening."

"Inclement! You vastly understate the matter, James. Why, I feared our carriage would be blown off the road," Lady Lynton declared.

"Indeed, and thinking of you children out in such a storm is enough to give one grey hairs," Marjorie added with a shudder. "I am only thankful I did not know of it sooner. Louisa and I waited at Lady Fitzhugh's until the worst of it was over and we arrived home only minutes before Serena."

"You will notice she was not worrying over *my* travelling through the storm," Sir Laurence said, grinning at James.

"No, and how should I be when I had no notion you were on the road? But it was a wonderful surprise," Marjorie added, her eyes full of love as she gazed adoringly at her husband.

"Papa's visit is one of the things we are celebrating, Jamie," Serena said, returning to her seat on the footstool drawn near her father.

James nodded and sat down next to his mother on the love-seat. He was vaguely aware of her hand smoothing the shoulder of his coat, but his eyes were on Serena.

"And, of course, your mama's arrival, too," she added, with a sweet smile for Lady Lynton. "It is almost like being at home."

Not quite, James thought. He could never remember his mother being on such intimate terms with the Trevelyans.

"And then there is Aunt Louisa's recovery," Serena was saying, counting off their good fortune on her fingers.

"I'll drink to that," Sylvester said, lifting his glass. "And don't forget our trip to Paris."

"As if anyone could, when it is all you have been talking about," Louisa scolded him. She turned to James. "We shall be taking an extensive trip abroad, and perhaps when you have time, you will advise us on the sort of accommodations we may expect."

"I should be glad to," James murmured, swirling the brandy in his glass. Then, inevitably, his eyes were drawn again to Serena. "You do have a great deal to celebrate."

"Oh, that is not all! There is Annie's return, and Doctor Pilman believes she will do very well after a day or two in bed."

"And Mrs. Moppit's dismissal," Marjorie added with a laugh.

"I wish you had been here, Jamie," Serena confided. "It was grand. Mrs. Moppit was furious when I brought Annie back and she said she would not stay in the same house with her. She is such a dreadful woman! Aunt Louisa simply told her we would miss her, though I shall not, and she left in a huff."

"I was just apologizing to your mama, James," Louisa added. "For Heaven only knows what sort of breakfast will be put before us tomorrow."

"You are staying here, then?" James asked his mother with some surprise.

"Lady Marcham has been kind enough to invite me, and I thought to accept, at least until I know what your plans are and how long you mean to remain in Town. I suppose I could open the house...."

"No, not unless you mean to stay without me. I am planning to return home next week."

"Alone?" his mother asked sharply, and was relieved at her son's nod.

Serena sat quietly, her mind whirling. Had Jamie quarrelled with the widow? Perhaps because he'd come to her rescue? She kept her eyes down, unable to look at him, and listened to the conversation floating about her.

She heard her mother telling Lady Lynton they, too, would be returning to Malmesbury the following week, but Jamie said nothing. She stole a peek at him from beneath her lashes and was troubled by the misery on his handsome face. For a moment, an agonizing moment, she feared he was pining for the widow and her heart turned cold.

At that moment the chandelier above them shook perilously, and Serena, with the others, stared upwards. The candles suddenly seemed impossibly bright and everything else in the room receded. She felt as though she were enveloped in a glowing aura. Knowledge beyond reason, beyond doubt, filled her soul, and she knew with unmistakable certainty that Jamie loved her above all others. Loved her and had come to propose. Serena blinked and the lights dimmed, returning to normal, but the feeling of euphoria remained within her.

Sylvester stared at the chandelier and shook his head. "Louisa, my dear, we must have that thing looked at. Never known it to shake so."

"Perhaps it was the storm," she replied doubtfully as she rose. "Well, it has been an exceedingly long day and I confess I am rather tired."

The gentlemen stood at once and Marjorie, too, pleaded fatigue. Lady Lynton yawned behind her and shook her head sadly. "Travel does so wear one out, especially at our age. The young people, now, they can gad about all day and night without feeling the effects," she said, and smiled fondly at Serena. "Come here, my dear, and give me a kiss before I retire. I was just telling Sir Laurence on the drive down that you are such a pretty-behaved girl, and quite like my very own daughter."

James was embarrassed by his mother's tactics. He stood awkwardly, not knowing where to look, but Sir Laurence clapped him on the back. "We could say the same about you, James. Now, I know Serena wishes to thank you for your help earlier this evening, so we'll leave you, but mind you do not keep her up too late."

Before James knew it, he found himself alone with Serena, save for a footman stationed in the hall near the open door. She had turned away from him, no doubt as embarrassed as he. He saw her shoulders shaking, and silently cursed his meddlesome mother for upsetting her. "Serena," he said softly, coming up behind her. "You must not mind what Mother says—"

"Oh, Jamie," she said, turning to him, her eyes brimming with laughter. "Was it not funny? I *am* sorry, and I know I should not laugh at your mother, but she is so droll."

"Minx! I thought you were upset. I shall not spare any more sympathy for you!"

"Oh, were you feeling sorry for me?" she asked, looking up at him mischievously. With the certain knowledge of his intentions, she could not resist teasing him. "You need not, Jamie. I am very, very happy to be going home, and if London was not all I expected it to be, well, it has at least given me a better appreciation for... for Malmesbury."

"Has it, my dear?"

Unnerved by the probing intensity of his eyes, she started to turn away from him, but Jamie held her shoulders firmly between his hands and she could not move—nor did she wish to.

"Serena..." he murmured, gazing down at her. He had to restrain a strong urge to lower his head and taste her delicate mouth.

"Yes, Jamie?" she said softly, her lips parting slightly.

He released her abruptly, stepping away from her. There were matters to be settled before he had the right to claim those lips, and he could not think clearly with her in his arms. He walked away from her and halted before the sofa. "Come sit down, my dear. There is something I wish to ask you, though I know I do not have the right."

"What is it, Jamie?" Serena questioned, her brows drawn together as she watched him. When he did not immediately reply, she sat down as he requested. "Surely we are such old friends that there is nothing you could not ask me."

"It is about Rotterdam," he said abruptly.

"Oh, Ivor," she replied with a smile. "I know you do not much admire him, Jamie, but I do think if you were better acquainted, you would agree he is a very good sort of person."

"I have no wish to know him better," he muttered, and then, realizing he was making a botch of it, began to pace the room.

Serena watched him for a moment, and when he halted by the window, rose and came to stand beside him. "Jamie? Did you mean it when you said you were returning home alone? I—I rather thought Mrs. Tallant would go with you."

"So, apparently, did my mother, but you were both wrong. The lady and I have parted company."

"Oh. I hope it was not because you came to my assistance tonight," she said, knowing it was not, but wanting to hear the words.

"No," he said, an ironic smile curling his lips as he recalled the scene with Beryl. "She did not object to that, though if she had, it would not have made any difference. There is not a person on Earth who could prevent me from coming to your aid if you needed me."

"Truly, Jamie?"

"Truly, minx," he said, and could not keep from reaching out and smoothing her hair. She turned her head quickly, and kissed the palm of his hand.

Serena heard him groan and smiled to herself as she stepped closer and laid her head against his shoulder. Her hand rested on his chest and she played with a button on his coat. "If you come whenever I need you, I fear it will be excessively awkward for you, for I find I need you constantly."

"Serena, you cannot know what you are saying," James murmured, his lips against her silky hair.

She felt his embrace tighten slightly, and could hear the hammering of his heart. "I do know, Jamie," she whispered. "And I do need you, every minute of every day."

James was incapable of resisting her further. He drew back slightly, and when Serena looked up, his lips came down on hers in a fiercely possessive kiss. His arms tightened about her and Serena lifted her hands to entwine them in his hair, returning his kiss with an ardour that took his breath away.

He lifted his head but kept her firmly in his embrace, and even then he could not resist kissing her brow and the indentation by her eye. "Serena, you must speak to your parents at once and tell them you cannot wed Rotterdam. I know it will be awkward for you to draw back now—"

"I never intended to wed Rotterdam," she interrupted, standing on the tips of her toes to place a gentle kiss on his lips. "How could I, Jamie, when my heart has always belonged to you?"

It took him a few seconds to realize what she had said. Then he swept her up in his arms, lifting her off the floor and kissing her again in earnest.

Lady Lynton, peeping silently in from the hall, smiled broadly and would have entered at once to congratulate her son had not Sir Laurence laid a firm hand on her arm and drawn her along to the sitting-room. "It appears Louisa was right about James, but there will be time enough tomorrow to discuss the wedding plans," he whispered.

"What is there to discuss?" she asked. "Of course they will be married in the chapel at Wynyard. Lyntons have been wed there since the first viscount in 1612. You may not be aware of it, Laurence, but it is a very old tradition in our family."

"I am aware of it, Henrietta, and I do not suppose either James or Serena will have any objection where they are wed, so long as it is soon."

"Yes, indeed it must be soon, for I have my daughter to attend to in December. Thank heavens they finally came to their senses."

THE THOUGHT WAS ECHOED by Cuthbert, reclining in the cushioned window-seat. He was content to watch the couple sitting close together by the dying fire, softly discussing their future. Serena was nestled in Jamie's arms, her head on his shoulder, her hand occasionally reaching up to caress his face. Cuthbert blinked and a lone teardrop slipped unnoticed down his cheek. "She will make a beautiful bride, Eleazar."

"She will indeed, Major, and I offer you my warmest congratulations."

"Well," Cuthbert owned gruffly, wiping away more tears and finding his throat suddenly tight, "I will admit manoeuvring the chandelier was going a bit beyond the line, but worth it, do you not think?"

"I do indeed, but I was not referring to Serena and James," Eleazar said with a tender smile. "Look at you, my friend. You have finally learned to love another more than yourself. Listen, Cuthbert."

He snapped his fingers, summoning a breeze that blew the window slightly open. The sound seemed to come from a great distance, but if one was quite still, one could clearly hear church bells ringing, musical chimes—peal after peal proclaiming their joyous message. Another angel had earned his wings.

WHO SAYS THE PAST IS OLD NEWS?

Harlequin Regency Romance is bringing the past to life with six exciting new books!

June marks the publication of our 100th title and an all-new concept. The REGENCY QUARTET brings you a collection of stories by well-known British authors, offering you hours of big-book enjoyment. And you'll be sure to fall in love with a simply divine comedy, A MATCH MADE IN HEAVEN, by reader favorite Jeanne Carmichael. And don't miss the latest from popular author Barbara Neil—GENTLEMAN ROGUE.

Feel the heat in July and August with sizzling Regency romances by Barbara Neil, Elizabeth Michaels, Winifred Witton and Brenda Hiatt.

Join us this summer and find out what's new!

Look for Harlequin Regency Romance wherever Harlequin books are sold.